SWEETNESS AND LIGHT

A SWEET COVE, MASSACHUSETTS

COZY MYSTERY

BOOK 5

J.A. WHITING

To hear about new books and book sales, please sign up for my mailing list at: www.jawhitingbooks.com

For my family, with love

CHAPTER 1

Ellie Roseland edged her van into a parking spot in the lot of the Sweet Cove Resort. She, her three sisters, and the family friend, Mr. Finch, got out and headed for the front door. A warm breeze off the ocean carried a salty scent and the sound of the waves crashing against the sandy beach filled the air.

The resort was set on acres of lush lawn on a bluff called Robin's Point overlooking the Atlantic Ocean. The resort consisted of a main hotel-spa and a number of small suites set in cottage style bungalows spread across the magnificently landscaped grounds. Shade trees and flowering shrubs and bushes dotted the lawns, and perennials and annual flowers spilled from manicured beds and ceramic pots.

Twenty-two-year-old Courtney looked longingly at the ocean waves crashing against the white sand beach below the bluff. "I'd love to jump right into the surf."

A second round of weather with temperatures in

the low nineties had descended on Sweet Cove, so Courtney had her hair pulled loosely up on top of her head and she wore a sleeveless, sea foam-green summer dress. "It's sooo hot." She fussed and wiped at her forehead with the back of her hand.

The air conditioning in Ellie's van had broken down just as the high temperatures hit and riding in the vehicle was like being in an airless, stifling, closed up box.

Angie's shirt stuck to her back from perspiration. She winced when she reached behind to pull the cloth away from her skin. Her shoulder and neck were still sensitive and sore from being hit by a baseball bat while she was trying to solve a recent crime.

"After this meeting," Jenna said, "let's head down to the beach for thirty minutes and swim before we all have to head off to work."

Despite the high temperatures, Mr. Finch was dressed in a pressed white shirt, necktie, and suit jacket. He leaned on his cane. "I must present a professional appearance to our new clients."

As the five of them approached the front entrance to the resort lobby, Josh Williams, the resort co-owner, came out to greet them. Angie quickly smoothed her honey-blonde hair and straightened her skirt attempting to look cool and calm. It was a losing battle since her internal temperature had increased a few degrees at the sight of the attractive man heading towards them.

Josh smiled broadly at Angie, bent, and kissed her sweetly. "How is your shoulder?" He brushed his hand over her arm being careful not to jostle her limb and cause her discomfort.

"It's getting better." *But not fast enough*, Angie thought. She was surprised at how long it was taking to regain the full use of her shoulder.

Josh said, "Senator Winston texted me and said that he and his daughter were running late. Would you like to come into the café and have a cold drink before they arrive?"

Everyone happily agreed and turned for the door just as Josh spotted the Winston vehicle heading their way from the parking area. "Oh, here they come now."

A powder blue Bentley convertible drove slowly around the circular entrance drive. A white-haired man sat in the driver's seat and a platinum blonde stared straight ahead from the passenger side, a bored expression on her face.

The man waved to Josh as they glided past. He called out. "We'll have to arrange another meeting time. Can't make it today." The young woman didn't even glance at the group. The vehicle picked up speed and headed away down the long driveway to the street.

Josh looked dumbfounded. "What the....?"

"Nice meeting you, too," Courtney deadpanned. "I guess our meeting has come to a close."

Josh apologized for dragging the Roselands and

Mr. Finch to the resort for nothing. "I suppose we'll reschedule." He scowled after the Bentley as it made a right turn from the driveway onto the main street.

Ellie grumped. "That was very rude." She crossed her arms in front of her chest. Ellie believed in good manners and courteous behavior.

"I guess Senators do things in their own time and in their own way." Jenna shrugged.

"*Former* Senator." Mr. Finch tapped his cane on the pavement. "Why don't we go inside and have that cold drink anyway. Miss Betty isn't picking me up for an hour." Mr. Finch was dating Sweet Cove's most successful real estate broker, Betty Hayes. Finch recently closed on the house located right behind Angie's Victorian, and with the help of the Roseland sisters, he had moved his few belongings into his new home. Finch and Betty were going furniture shopping later in the day.

The four sisters, Mr. Finch, and Josh headed out of the oppressive heat and into the air conditioned coolness of the resort hotel. Senator Winston and his daughter Bethany were supposed to meet to go over her wedding plans and make arrangements with Angie for the cake and other desserts for the reception, discuss the choice of treats for the gift bags from Courtney and Finch's confectioner store, review jewelry designs with Jenna for the wedding party, and talk about retaining Ellie as a wedding consultant to assist in the orchestration of the quickly approaching event.

"The Winstons haven't started off by making a very good impression." Angie shook her head. She couldn't help but smile at the behavior of the Winston father and daughter. She was more amused than annoyed about the meeting being blown off and she wondered if she wasn't bothered because she was now in such lovely air-conditioned surroundings with handsome Josh Williams by her side.

The group walked through the elegantly decorated lobby and into the café where they settled into comfortable chairs around a table set next to floor-to-ceiling windows which afforded a beautiful view of the grounds and out over the ocean. A waiter brought cold drinks and a variety of appetizers to snack on.

"I'm starving." Courtney transferred some stuffed mushrooms, triangles of spanakopita, and several wedges of cheese to her appetizer plate.

"No one is surprised at that." Jenna's blue eyes sparkled as she kidded her youngest sister, but then she followed Courtney's example by reaching for some of the tasty treats.

"What can you tell us about the Winstons and their expectations for the wedding?" Ellie sipped sparkling water from her glass.

Josh put his fork on his plate. "Senator Winston served in government for several years representing a Midwestern state. I can't remember which one at the moment. He worked as an investment banker prior to running for the Senate seat. He claimed to miss the business and so, retired from Congress to return to banking. They are a very wealthy family. I was surprised to hear that they wanted to hold the wedding in Sweet Cove. I'm pleased, of course, but its all so last minute that it will cause some problems, what with shifting guests around and planning the entire event so quickly." Josh took a swallow of his iced tea. "As you probably gathered, Senator Winston is quite demanding and doesn't handle disappointment well. We'll have to be on our toes so everything goes the way he wants it."

"What about the daughter?" Angie asked. "Has she voiced her preferences?"

Josh didn't answer right away which sent a little skitter of unease over Angie's skin.

"She never says much. She acts, sort of bored by the whole thing."

Ellie narrowed her eyes. "How very odd."

"Do you get any sense of why she is so reserved about the planning?" Jenna wondered what the reason could be for Bethany Winston's reticence.

Courtney held her fork suspended over her plate. "I think it would be fun to plan my wedding." She grinned. "I'd have all kinds of opinions about how things should be."

"Is the young lady's mother giving input about the wedding plans?" Mr. Finch looked thoughtful.

"Mrs. Winston passed away when Bethany was a

little girl." Josh glanced at the waiter and called him over to replenish the drinks and snacks. "The Senator told me that it's just himself and his daughter, no other relatives."

The Roseland sisters lost their father when they were small and their mother passed away from an accident just a few years ago. Angie offered, "Maybe the man just wants to make everything perfect for his daughter."

"And, maybe he's smothering her." Jenna shrugged her shoulder. "Maybe the Senator needs to back off a little."

"What about the groom?" Ellie questioned Josh. "Have you met him?"

Josh shook his head. "His name is Nelson Rider. They told me he is on a business trip to Asia. They don't have a firm date for his return."

"It will be *before* the wedding, though, right?" Courtney joked.

Josh grinned. "I didn't think to ask that question."

"Well." Mr. Finch clasped his hands. "If nothing else, this business arrangement is going to prove interesting."

"Working with the Winstons probably isn't going to be all sweetness and light," Ellie noted, brushing her long blonde hair over her shoulder. "But considering everything else we've dealt with since moving to Sweet Cove, I think we can handle them."

A flicker of discomfort shivered down Angie's

spine. She certainly hoped they could.

spine. She certainly hoped they could.

CHAPTER 2

Angie and Jenna hunched over the jewelry desks in the shop at the back of the Victorian. Jenna was finishing the last sketch of several necklace ideas that she'd come up with for the Winston wedding party. She held it up for her sister to see. "What do you think?"

Angie oohed. "I love it. It's my favorite of all the designs you've done to show Bethany Winston." She bent to finish the bracelet she was working on. "Don't give away your best designs. Save some for my wedding."

"I might be an old woman by the time you get married." Jenna chuckled.

Angie ignored her.

Jenna rubbed at a kink in her neck and watched her sister. "You've gotten faster making the jewelry."

"I am a production machine." Angie lifted a tool from the desk to clamp a bead.

Jenna eyed the bracelet. "And the quality?"

"Well, the quality has slipped with my

increasing speed." Angie teased.

"I might have to fire you." Jenna rested her chin in her hand.

"You mean I'll go from working for you for no pay, to *not* working for you for no pay? I sure wouldn't want that to happen." Angie smiled and eyed her fraternal twin sister. "Don't worry. The quality remains high."

Ellie came into the room carrying a tray with three lattes on it. She put one on each desk and took the third cup with her to the sofa where she took a seat in between the two cats. She had to push Euclid's huge orange plume of a tail to the side so she could sit.

"So, what do you think of the Winston wedding?" Ellie sipped her beverage.

Angie sighed. "I don't know what to think." She'd told her sisters and Mr. Finch that she'd felt some pangs of anxiety when Josh was telling them about Senator Winston and his daughter. "I hope this isn't going to be a pain. They are probably going to be very demanding clients."

"Well, one of them will be." Jenna was not looking forward to the father and his stipulations. "But maybe I'll only be dealing with Bethany since I'm handling the jewelry side of things."

Ellie grunted. "Oh, I'm sure daddy dear will have plenty of opinions about what sort of baubles will be adorning the wedding party."

Angie strung a few stones onto the beading wire.

"We didn't learn much about Bethany." She peered over at Jenna and smiled. "Since you're not doing anything, Sis, why don't you look her up on the internet?"

Jenna tapped on her laptop. "I'm going to look up Senator Winston first. Why didn't I think to do this before?" She clicked on one of the entries that came up in the search and after reading a few lines, she let out a little yelp. "This guy is loaded." She eyed her sisters with a sly grin. "The prices that we're going to charge Senator Winston for our services have just quadrupled."

"What does it say about him?" Ellie stroked Circe's black fur.

Jenna paraphrased what was on the screen. "His net worth is 2.3 *billion* dollars."

Angie dropped the tool she'd been holding. She blinked at her sister. "You're kidding."

Jenna continued reading. "Norman Winston graduated from Harvard Business School and Harvard Law School. He donated thirty million dollars to his alma mater for a new building project."

"How did he make his money?" Ellie asked.

"Investment banking." Jenna scanned the online article for more information about the man. "He has one child, Bethany. He had a brother and a sister, but they've both passed away. His wife, Candace, passed away suddenly and unexpectedly when the daughter was only four."

A sudden chill ran through Angie's stomach. "Does it say what the cause of death was?"

"Heart attack." Jenna peered at the screen. "Winston served one term in the Senate and then returned to banking. That's about it."

"Look up the daughter."

Euclid had moved onto Ellie's lap and was stretched out over her with his head hanging down on one side against the sofa and his long legs dangling over her right hip. His feet pressed against Circe's side. Since the black cat was accustomed to the huge orange boy taking up most of the space, she didn't react to Euclid pushing against her.

Jenna read aloud from the computer screen. "So this is like a repeat of the father. Bethany graduated from Harvard Law and works in Boston for a prominent firm. There isn't much else about her. She's twenty-nine years old."

"What about the groom? Can you find anything on him?" Ellie was alternating her patting between the two cats. "Didn't Josh say his name was Nelson something?"

Jenna tapped. "Nelson Rider. Here we go." She read for a few moments. "Another prominent family. Seems like these people are even wealthier than Senator Winston. Nelson works at the family company. Some sort of venture capital thing, whatever that means. Worth billions." Jenna looked at her sisters. "Why aren't we worth billions?"

"We took a wrong turn somewhere." Angie chuckled. Her phone buzzed and she reached for it to see the incoming text. "It's Josh. Bethany would like to come here and meet with Jenna about the jewelry."

"When?" Jenna asked.

Angie looked up. "She's on her way."

Jenna squawked, "What?!"

The three girls flew into action cleaning and straightening up the jewelry room. Beads and silver findings were shoved into drawers. Ellie zoomed around the room with the vacuum. The cats were shooed away and Angie ran a lint roller over the sofa to remove the creatures' hair.

Jenna set her sketch book on the round table near the fireplace, put suede mats down, and placed examples of the different necklace designs on the mats. When she was satisfied with the display, she ran to her room to change and brush her hair, while Angie brought a vase of flowers into the room from the dining table and Ellie hurried to the kitchen to make iced tea and arrange some of the B and B's morning breakfast treats on a serving dish. Jenna was just coming back down the stairs to the foyer when the doorbell rang.

Angie opened the Victorian's front door to find a tall, slender platinum blonde standing on the porch. Her hair was cut in a short chin-length bob with bangs. She had huge brown eyes. A tight, caramel-colored skirt accentuated her fit figure. The young woman extended her hand to shake with Angie. "Hello. I'm Bethany Winston, here to see Jenna Roseland."

Angie introduced herself and stepped back to allow the woman to enter.

Jenna had her long brown hair held back in a ponytail and she had on a pale blue summer dress and navy sandals. She welcomed Bethany and led her to her shop at the back of the house.

"What a lovely Victorian home." Bethany glanced around the foyer and dining room as she followed Jenna down the hall. "You've decorated it perfectly."

Angie heard the comment and smiled. She wanted to stand outside the door to Jenna's shop so she could eavesdrop on their conversation. As she followed Jenna and Bethany Winston down the hall and past the kitchen doorway, Ellie stood there with a serious expression on her face and her arms crossed over her chest. "Do not stand outside Jenna's door."

"I wasn't going to." Angie put on an offended face, but she was really only put out because Ellie had caught her.

"Come in here and help me set up a tray." Ellie turned.

Angie sighed and followed her sister into the kitchen. As she was removing the iced tea from the refrigerator, her phone buzzed with a text from

Josh. Angie looked up, confused. "It's from Josh. Senator Winston is on his way here to talk to me about the wedding cake. He also wants to discuss the event with the wedding consultant." Angie made eye contact with Ellie. "That would be you."

"Why didn't he come with Bethany? This is one strange group." Ellie rolled her eyes. "And, have none of these people ever heard of making an appointment before showing up?"

Angie's phone buzzed with another text and she flicked her eyes to the screen. "The groom, Nelson Rider, is accompanying the Senator."

***

Ellie and Angie changed clothes so they wouldn't look like wrecks when they met the Senator and the bridegroom. They thought they'd better warn Bethany about the impending visit by the men, so they both carried some treats into the jewelry shop.

"How are things going?" Ellie smiled and placed a tray with iced tea, sparkling water, and two glasses on the table.

"We thought you might like some refreshments." Angie put the glass plate of different squares and mini Danish next to the beverage tray.

"We're just looking at the sketches and going over design possibilities." Jenna turned to her client. "Would you like something to drink?"

Bethany, leaning over the sketches, requested

some sparkling water.

"I just had a text from the resort." Angie poured the water. "Your father and fiancé are on their way over here."

Bethany's head jerked up and her face hardened. With her hands on the table, she pushed out of her seat with force. Ramming her hand into her blazer pocket, she retrieved her car keys which she shoved at Angie. "Move my car around the block." Bethany turned to the door that led to the wraparound porch. "Don't tell them I was here. Can I go out this door?" Not waiting for an answer, she bolted for the exit.

Jenna stood and pointed. "Go through the trees at the back of the yard. You'll come out in the next yard. Our friend lives there. Cut over to the street."

Bethany was gone in a flash.

"Quick. Move the car." Ellie gave Angie a gentle push to the door.

Angie took off through the exit and ran to Bethany's car in the driveway.

No one knew why there was such a rush to cover for Bethany, but the girls were caught up by the urgency and fell in to help. Jumping into the driver's seat of the Porsche and backing it out to the street, Angie wondered why on earth anyone would run away from her fiancé.

CHAPTER 3

After delivering the car to Bethany on the next street over, Angie walked home and opened the door to Jenna's shop. The room was empty so she headed down the hallway to the foyer. Hearing voices coming from the sunroom, she went in that direction and saw Ellie chatting with Senator Winston and a young man who Angie assumed was Nelson Rider, the fiancé.

Ellie looked relieved when she spotted her sister entering the room. "This is my sister, Angie."

The two men, wearing what looked like expensive fitted suits, stood and shook hands with the newcomer.

The sunroom had three walls of glass with long, wide windows that opened to let in the breeze. The walls were cream and three pale mocha sofas were positioned in a U-shape around a blonde wooden coffee table. Plants with deep green foliage stood here and there around the room in ceramic pots.

Angie sat down on one of the empty sofas and noticed the cats sitting on the glass side table in the far corner of the room. They were scowling at the guests.

"We're just going over some details for the wedding." Ellie informed her sister with one raised eyebrow which clued Angie in that something was odd.

"Is Bethany here?" Angie asked innocently knowing full well that the young woman had just escaped.

"No, it's just the two gentlemen." Ellie smiled sweetly. She had a notebook balanced on one knee and held a silver pen.

Angie decided to question the men and turned to them with a pleasant smile on her face. "Shouldn't you wait for the bride's input?"

Nelson Rider gave what the sisters would classify as a fake smile. His teeth were blazing white and perfectly aligned. "That isn't necessary." His sandy-blonde hair was cut close to his head. He gave the impression of a body full of suppressed energy, as if, at the least provocation, he would rise and go outside to run a marathon.

Everything about this guy was perfect. His haircut. Posture. Clothing, well-made and perfectly tailored. His manners. His diction. Angie wondered if he ever perspired, or tripped, or misspoke. She thought he seemed like a spring that was wound too tight.

"But," Angie persisted. "The bride is usually a big part of a wedding."

"Bethany likes what I like." Nelson was still smiling.

"Do *you* like what she likes?" Angie asked. She wondered if Bethany was always bending to Nelson's wishes while Nelson made all the decisions without considering her wants or feelings.

Nelson looked confused.

"You're the baker, correct?" Senator Winston inquired. He leaned back against the sofa like he owned the place. One arm lay across the sofa back in a wide, relaxed gesture.

Angie nodded.

"I'd like to see some examples of cakes you've created. Then we can choose what we like and discuss flavors."

Angie bristled. "I'll need your daughter's preferences before finalizing things."

The Senator pooh-poohed that comment. "Bethany will be absolutely fine with whatever Nelson and I choose."

Angie scowled and was about to respond when Ellie piped up. "I think it best if we wait to continue when Bethany can join us. We can all meet together very soon to finish up the details."

The men were about to protest, but Ellie stood up and took a few steps towards the doorway. "I have another client now," she lied. "You have my number. Give me a call to arrange a time when everyone is available." She gestured towards the front of the house and the men reluctantly got up and headed for the Victorian's front door.

When Ellie shut it after the men, she wheeled towards Angie. "They hardly even mentioned Bethany. It's like they're creating some show or spectacle and she is only to play a part."

Euclid and Circe sat on the bottom step of the staircase. Euclid released a low hiss from deep in his throat and Circe emitted a growl.

Ellie's face was flushed and her arms flailed as she gestured animatedly. "I don't think I can work with them."

Jenna heard her younger sister ranting and came into the foyer to find out what was happening. The girls relayed the strangeness of the brief meeting.

"Well, that's as odd as the bride scooting out the door when her dear fiancé is about to show up." Jenna narrowed her eyes. "What do you think is going on here?"

The three of them headed for the family room with the cats tailing after them. Ellie started up a new rant as they walked into the room. Jenna and Angie took seats on the sofa just as Courtney came in from the back door of the house. "What's cookin'?"

"Plenty." Ellie paced around the family room as she complained about Senator Winston and Nelson Rider and relayed how Bethany ran through the backyard to leave the house before the men showed up.

Courtney's eyes went wide listening to what went on during the meetings. "I wasn't expecting this."

"Ellie doesn't want to work with them." Jenna stretched out on the sofa and put her legs over Angie's lap.

Courtney sat in the easy chair and tucked her legs up under herself. "I don't agree. What does it matter to us if they're nuts or weird or whatever. It's business. People at the wedding might like what we do and hire us for another event. One thing can lead to another. I'd be happy to make candy for the Winston wedding. If their strange behavior works for them, then what do we care?"

Ellie stopped her hurried pacing from one side of the room to the other and stared at Courtney.

"The voice of reason." Jenna chuckled.

Ellie plopped onto the opposite sofa. Her brow furrowed. "I guess you're right."

"Okay. That's settled." Courtney got up. "Let's make dinner." She headed for the kitchen.

"Bah." Jenna pushed herself up and followed her sister, muttering. "I thought we were going to sit for a while."

Mr. Finch sat at the kitchen table with a cup of tea, reading the newspaper. Even though Finch was living in his own house now, he was an adopted member of the Roseland family, coming and going as he pleased and often eating his meals with the sisters. He looked up when the girls came in.

"Did you pick out some furniture this

afternoon?" Angie asked.

"Indeed, I did. Miss Betty and I visited the store in West Cove and I picked out some things for the living room, a dining room set, and a bedroom set. I am quite happy with my choices. The new things will be delivered later in the week. In due time, I will furnish the upstairs rooms, but there's no rush."

"I can't wait to see what you bought." Courtney smiled at Finch.

"I saw the strangest thing this afternoon." Finch adjusted his eyeglasses. "A young woman, blonde, quite attractive, came running through the wooded area between our two houses. I wondered if you were chasing your bed and breakfast guests away from the premises."

Angie grinned. "That was Bethany Winston. She escaped from a meeting with Jenna." She gave her sister a mock questioning look. "Maybe Bethany didn't like anything she saw in your shop?"

Jenna ignored Angie's comment and clarified for Mr. Finch what had happened.

"How very odd." The man tilted his head in a questioning posture. Circe jumped on his lap and curled up. Finch scratched her cheek. "It seems clear that Ms. Winston is not very fond of her fiancé."

Ellie sat down across from Finch. "Then why do you think she is marrying him?"

"There could be a number of reasons." The older

man's forehead creased. "There probably aren't many men of such means. The Winstons must have a very small social circle of families of their position and wealth. It could be that Ms. Winston does not wish to marry outside of that circle. Maybe she has known the young man since she was a small girl and they get along, but she really doesn't love him. It could be a marriage of convenience for both of them, two very powerful families joining together."

"That's sad." Ellie frowned.

"Maybe it isn't." Courtney lifted the lid on the crockpot and checked the simmering meat, and then she went to wash lettuce at the sink. "Maybe it's just what super rich people do."

"Then I'm glad I'm not wealthy." Ellie's eyes clouded. She got up, left the kitchen, and walked to the dining room to set the table.

"I wish I was wealthy." Courtney ladled the beef stew from the crock pot into a blue and white serving bowl. "I prefer love *and* money."

CHAPTER 4

Courtney snuggled in the easy chair with Euclid who lay next to her sound asleep with his head hanging off the seat cushion. Ellie sat on the loveseat with Circe curled in her lap. Angie was supposed to be watching the movie, but she'd dozed off. Jenna sat with Angie on the sofa and because the air conditioner was going full blast, she pulled a blanket over her lap rather than turn it down because the cool air felt so good.

Just as an important scene from the film was playing on the screen, Euclid bolted up and let out a hiss, waking Angie and causing the other girls to jump. Circe stared at the orange cat and then she cocked her head focusing on the sound that had alerted Euclid.

The doorbell rang and everyone startled.

"Who could this be?" Ellie didn't want to go to the door because she was wearing old shorts and a faded t-shirt. "It's eleven at night. It can't be one of the B and B guests. I gave everyone the code to the front door."

Angie lifted her head from the sofa, looking disoriented. She blinked and rubbed her eyes.

"It must be someone who forgot the code. Again." Jenna pushed the blanket to one side and stood up. "I'll go see." She hurried down the hall to the foyer.

The cats were on full alert. They jumped down and followed Jenna into the hall and raced her to the front door. The bell rang again.

"I'm coming, for Pete's sake." Jenna muttered under her breath before swinging the front door open.

Bethany Winston stood under the porch light, her platinum hair glowing from the illumination. Taking a glance over her shoulder to the dark street, she hurried into the Victorian without being invited to enter. "I need to speak with you and your sisters."

Jenna started, "It's really not a good time...."

Bethany cut her off. "It's very important. I'll try to take only a bit of your evening."

Jenna thought, the *evening* is already over, it's *night* now, but she didn't say so.

Circe and Euclid watched warily from the staircase, listening.

"Um." Jenna looked down the hallway. "We're relaxing in the family room. We're not really presentable for guests."

Bethany moved her hand dismissively. "I don't care what you look like. I just want to talk." Her big, brown eyes looked hopefully at Jenna. "It's important."

Jenna stifled a sigh from escaping from her throat. "Why don't you have a seat in the living room for a few minutes. Let me go tell my sisters that you're here." She walked down the hallway and into the family room.

Angie was still stretched out on the sofa and had her eyes closed. Ellie and Courtney were focused on the movie that was playing on the television.

Ellie didn't move her eyes from the screen. "Who was it?"

"Bethany Winston."

The television watchers turned towards Jenna.

"She's in the living room. She needs to talk to us, she says it's important."

Angie groaned without opening her eyes. "You three go."

"Really? She's here so late." Courtney stood up, her face bright with interest. "What's it about?"

Jenna shrugged and turned back to the hall. "Let's go find out. You too, Angie."

"Bah." Angie muttered and swung her legs off the sofa.

When the four girls were at the threshold of the living room, Bethany jumped up from her seat. Her words tumbled out in a rush. "Thank you for seeing me. I apologize for running off like that earlier today. There's something I need to talk to you about."

Everyone sat down. The cats watched the woman from their position in front of the fireplace. Ellie hoped that this intrusion into their free time wasn't about some small wedding detail that could wait until tomorrow.

Bethany seemed to be struggling with what to say. She fidgeted on the sofa and her expression was tight and tense.

"What would you like to speak with us about?" Angie gave a small encouraging smile trying to prompt her.

Bethany exhaled loudly. "I don't know where to start."

"What's bothering you?" Jenna asked.

"Many things." The platinum blonde shook her head, and then made eye contact with the four sisters. "I read about you in the newspapers. I need your help."

Angie groaned inwardly. In her head, she cursed the news outlets. The very words that Bethany had just uttered had preceded a development in the sisters' last murder case. Angie braced herself.

Bethany went on. "I have a friend."

The girls waited for more.

"He and I have been friends since grade school." Bethany clasped her hands in her lap. Her brow furrowed. "I'm very worried about him."

"What seems to be the trouble?" Jenna leaned slightly forward.

"He is going to be my "Man of Honor" or "Best

Man" or whatever words would be appropriate for a bride to have a male friend as her "Maid of Honor."

Ellie bristled, but remained quiet, annoyed that semantics was the cause of this late night visit. She wondered why the appropriate term to use for the man standing up for Bethany at her wedding couldn't be discussed during the day.

Bethany eyes watered. "Something happened. His life has been threatened."

"Just because he's going to be your Best Man?" Ellie gaped.

"No." The young woman shook her head. "I don't know. That can't be the whole reason. I need you to figure this out."

Angie swallowed. "Have the police been told about the threat?"

Bethany sighed and shook her head. "We haven't told anyone."

"Why not?" Jenna's eyes narrowed.

"We don't want any unnecessary publicity."

"But if the threat is real...." Courtney said.

"That's why I'm coming to you first. If you can't find any clues, then we'll go to the police."

"How was the threat presented?" Angie questioned.

"My friend has received several letters, two in the mail and one on his doorstep. There are cut up letters from a magazine that spell out the message, just like in a movie." She wrung her hands.

"When did the first one arrive?" Jenna asked.

"Four weeks ago."

"Was your wedding date common knowledge then?" Courtney tried to make a connection between the timing of the threats and what might have precipitated the warning letters.

"The first letter arrived just prior to when our save-the-date announcements went out."

"What did the letter say?" Ellie looked like she didn't really want to know.

Bethany cleared her throat. "It said, 'I know you love Bethany. Enjoy your last days on Earth.'"

Four pairs of eyes widened. Ellie covered her mouth with her hand.

"Is that true? *Does* he love you?" Courtney sat up straighter, intrigued by a possible love triangle.

Bethany gave a slight nod and looked at the floor. "And I love him," she said softly.

After a full minute of silence, Angie stood up slowly. "Let's have some tea and something to eat. Why don't we move to the family room where it's more private, in case other guests show up and want to use these rooms?"

"Do you have any wine?" Bethany asked. Her face was pale and she looked a little shaky.

Just as everyone stood up to follow Angie to the hall, some B and B guests opened the front door and entered. They greeted the group as they passed each other and the guests moved to the buffet table in the dining room to sample the evening treats and sit around the table and chat. Angie was glad they'd decided to move to a quieter room in order to talk openly. Once settled in the family room with tea and wine and some shortbread wedges, the questions started up again.

"Is it commonly known that you and this man have a thing?" Courtney asked.

Bethany's eyes flashed. "We don't' have a *thing*."

"Okay, poor choice of word." Courtney corrected herself. "Do people know that you and this man have affection for one another?"

"People know that we're friends."

"Did you ever date the man?" Ellie held her mug on her knee.

Bethany vigorously shook her head. "Father would have had a fit."

"So nobody knows that you both harbor feelings for one another?" Jenna was trying to paint a picture of the relationship and what others might know or suspect about them. "Except for the person who sent the threatening letters."

"People know we're friends," Bethany repeated.

Ellie didn't think they were getting enough information. "Can you tell us about your interactions with this man? How often do you see him? Where does he live? Do you socialize together? Things like that? What's his name?"

Angie looked at her sister, impressed at what a good detective she was turning out to be.

Bethany seemed to wrestle with revealing the details of the situation, probably because she was afraid to disclose particulars of the "friendship." She rested back against the sofa. "His name is Todd Moore. He lives in Boston. He works as a teacher. He volunteers at an animal shelter. Todd runs marathons, enjoys camping and hiking. Things I'd never done before. My father would rather die than take part in such activities." She sipped some wine. "Todd and I have always gotten along perfectly, we understand each other. He cares about me." Tears started to fall and Ellie passed the young woman some tissues.

"Why are you marrying someone else if you love Todd?" Courtney wanted to hear the explanation to the question that was on everyone's lips.

Bethany dabbed at her eyes. "My father would kill Todd if he knew I loved him."

Four pairs of eyes bugged out of their respective sockets. The words *kill Todd* echoed in the sisters' heads.

CHAPTER 5

Angie tried to keep her voice even. "Is your comment an exaggeration or do you really feel that your father would hurt Todd because you are in love with each other?"

Bethany sat quietly picking at her tissue considering Angie's question.

"Could your father be the one who sent those letters to Todd?" Courtney's eyes were like saucers. She wondered if Senator Winston was truly a dangerous man.

"It's possible." Bethany's voice was soft and low. "But I don't think he did."

"Could he just be trying to frighten Todd off? He wouldn't really harm him, would he?" Ellie hoped she was right.

Bethany shrugged. "My father has some powerful contacts. He doesn't have to get his hands dirty when there's a problem."

Ellie nearly jumped out of her chair. "Has your father caused harm to people?" Her voice was shrill.

"I don't think so." Bethany didn't make eye contact. "He certainly hasn't killed anyone."

"Where is Todd now?" Jenna wanted to change the subject so that Ellie wouldn't run off.

"He's in Sweet Cove. He's staying at an inn near the beach. He arrived this evening. I haven't seen him yet." Bethany let out a sigh. "What a mess my life is."

Angie asked, "Why is Todd here?"

Bethany's long lashes blinked over her eyes. "He is my Best Man. He's going to help me with the wedding details."

"You're kidding." Courtney was aghast. "You love each other and he is going to help you plan your wedding to another man?"

Bethany just looked at Courtney with sad eyes. Dark circles showed under her lower lids.

Courtney ran her hands through her hair. "You didn't really answer my earlier question. Why are you marrying Nelson Rider if you don't love him?"

Bethany's shoulders slouched making her look small and fragile. It was a strange contrast to the confidant, assured woman who had appeared at the Victorian earlier that day. "My father thinks it's a good match."

Angie's phone buzzed on the side table next to her. She reached for it, stood up, and took the call out in the hallway.

Courtney pressed. "But *you* don't think Nelson is a good match. You're letting your father make one of your biggest life decisions for you. Maybe you can't marry Todd Moore right now, but you don't have to marry Nelson."

Angie came back into the room. Her shoulders were pulled up close to her neck and her lips were pressed together in two tight, thin lines. Jenna knew something was wrong, and she didn't have to see Angie to know. She could feel it floating in the air. "What was the call about?"

"We all need to go down to the resort." Angie swallowed hard and took a quick glance at Bethany.

"Now?" Ellie frowned. "It's so late. What on earth for? Who called you?"

"Josh called. We need to go. Now. He'll explain when we get there." She turned for the door and spoke to Bethany over her shoulder. "I didn't tell Josh that you're here." She quickly left the family room with the others staring after her.

Slowly everyone rose from their seats and headed for the hall.

"What's going on?" Bethany's voice shook. "Is something wrong? Why do you have to go to the resort at this hour?"

"I guess we'll find out when we get there." Jenna waited for the young woman to head for the foyer. As everyone gathered their things, Jenna sidled up next to her twin sister and whispered. "What's happened?"

Angie gave Jenna a serious look and checked that Bethany was out of ear-shot. "It's about

34

Bethany's fiancé. Nelson Rider. He's dead."

***

When the sisters were seated in Ellie's van and driving down Main Street, Angie told them the news about Bethany's fiancé, which caused Ellie to nearly lose control of the vehicle for a few moments. A barrage of questions hit Angie.

"Who found him? Are there signs of foul play? When did it happen? How long has he been dead?"

Angie told the girls that Josh didn't provide any details and only asked that the four of them come to the resort per request of Chief Martin.

Bethany, still in the dark about why they were called to the resort, drove her Porsche down the streets of Sweet Cove following behind Ellie's van. When the cars turned into the resort's parking lot, they could see the blue flashing lights of several police cars.

Ellie eased the van into a parking space and the sisters emerged. Bethany pulled into a spot on the other side of the lot. She told the girls before leaving the Victorian that she would park away from them and walk inside on her own because she didn't want to alert people that she had been with them.

A small crowd of people had gathered in front of the resort to watch what was happening. An officer, stationed at the door, would only allow registered guests to enter the lobby. When the young policeman saw the Roseland sisters approach, he waved them forward and opened the door to usher them inside.

Another patrolman nodded to the girls and asked them to follow him as he moved quickly down the main hotel hallway and out the door that led to the luxury bungalows.

"Where is he taking us?" Ellie's face was pale and she focused her eyes downward. She kept her voice soft. "I don't want to see a dead body. Who knows what happened to Nelson Rider. I can't look at a gruesome scene."

Jenna slipped her arm through her sister's. "He must be in his room. You can stand outside if you want to. No one will force you to see anything you don't want to look at." She could hear Ellie's rapid breathing.

They walked along tree-lined stone pathways to the section of the property where the exclusive bungalows were located. When they rounded a corner, they could see a crowd of people gathered in front of two of the cottages. The flashes of cameras reflected out of one of the suite's doors and washed over some of the people milling about outside. Chief Martin was standing next to a man in a suit conversing intently. He spotted the sisters, and moved away from the man towards the girls.

"So here we have the latest problem in Sweet Cove." The chief rubbed his forehead. He looked exhausted. "It's just been one thing after another lately." He gestured for the girls to enter the bungalow that stood next door to the murder scene cottage. "We're using this suite for law enforcement."

Inside in the living room area of the suite, there was a plush furniture grouping of sofas and chairs. They all sat. Police and detectives and tech assistants stood around the space in small groups, talking. "I'd prefer to go into one of the hotel conference rooms to chat, but I need to be visible in case I'm needed." Chief Martin made eye contact with each of the sisters. "Let's keep our voices down."

"What's happened?" Angie asked.

"As Josh informed you, Nelson Rider is dead. I told Josh I needed all of you here because you've been trained in grief counseling. I had to come up with something. Josh would have wondered why I was calling you to the scene." The chief seemed drained of his energy. "This is going to be a circus. A wealthy guy like this ... the media is going to be all over it. We can't make any mistakes. Don't speak with reporters. If they ask you questions, just say "no comment" and keep walking. Don't engage."

The girls nodded.

"Rider was shot. Once in the head. The killer put a pillow over Rider's face and head in order to muffle the gunshot. There was no sign that Rider resisted, so we assume he was asleep when the assailant came in. Housekeeping went into the bungalow to do their thing and found him."

"What time did they find him?" Jenna held her hands in her lap.

"Housekeeping starts doing the "turn-down" service around eight. They fold down the bed covers and put a candy on the pillow. You know what it is. Mr. Rider didn't want the turn-down service until after ten each night. So, one of the staff goes in around 10:45, finds him, goes hysterical. Josh was called, the police, the ambulances came. The housekeeper couldn't be calmed down so she was taken to the hospital. No witnesses. The surveillance cameras are being confiscated, but if the perpetrator went out the back then we're out of luck. The cameras are only trained on the front of the structures. Hotel staff members are being questioned right now ... inside the resort in a couple of conference rooms."

"No suspects as yet?" Courtney asked.

Chief Martin shook his head.

Angie suddenly thought of Bethany. "What about the Winstons? Who is breaking the news to them?"

"A police detective is the lucky holder of that job." The chief's lips turned down. The wrinkles around his eyes were more pronounced.

"What about Nelson's family?" Jenna asked.

"Rider has a sister in New York and a brother in

Boston." Chief Martin rubbed his eyes. The murders of the past months were taking a toll on the man.

The girls exchanged looks. Angie cleared her throat. "Bethany Winston was at our house when I got the call from Josh to come down here to the resort."

"So I guess she isn't on the suspect list." Jenna watched the law enforcement agents coming and going.

"Why was she at your house?" The chief's eyebrows bunched together.

The girls shifted uncomfortably in their seats. Finally Angie spoke. "She came to tell us that she is in love with someone other than her fiancé."

Courtney leaned forward and kept her voice low. "Bethany told us that her *friend*...." She raised an eyebrow to emphasize the word. "Has recently received letters threatening his life."

Chief Martin was about to say something when a plainclothes detective came around the corner from the small kitchen area and gestured to him. Chief Martin stood up. "Can you stay?" he asked the girls. "I'd like to hear more about this friend." He lowered his voice. "I'd also like you to take a look at the body and see the bungalow, if you'd be willing." He excused himself and followed after the detective.

"The plot thickens." Courtney narrowed her eyes. "Bethany is supposed to get married, but loves someone else, and then her fiancé is murdered." She tapped her finger against her chin. "How convenient."

Ellie's jaw dropped. "I didn't think of that. You think she set Rider up?"

"Did the *friend* have a hand in Nelson's murder?" Jenna had an expression of suspicion on her face. "Bethany told us that her friend just arrived in Sweet Cove this evening." She glanced at Courtney. "Is that a red herring? Was he in town earlier than she said? Did he happen to pay a visit to Nelson Rider?"

"Huh," Angie pondered. "Eliminate the fiancé and the troubles are over, right? Chief Martin needs to talk to Bethany and her friend. What was his name? Moore, something or other?"

"Todd Moore." Courtney pulled out her phone. "I'm going to look him up."

Ellie turned to Angie. "I don't want to see the body. Maybe looking at the suite would be okay, but definitely not the body." She gave a vigorous shake of her head. "Nuh-uh." She glanced around at the official-looking people hurrying back and forth from the scene of the crime to the suite they were sitting in. "I'd really like to go home." She looked at Jenna. "Can I go home? You three are better at this stuff than I am."

Angie turned her hands out, palms up, and gave a little shrug. "I don't know. I suppose it would be okay for you to leave. We can explain your absence to the chief. He'll understand."

Ellie's forehead scrunched. "Oh, but you'll have no way to get home if I leave."

"Chief Martin will drive us. Or a patrolman. Go ahead. Don't worry." Jenna encouraged her sister to head home. She knew that this kind of thing caused Ellie great distress and she didn't like to see her sister so uncomfortable. Jenna smiled. "Tell the cats what's going on."

Ellie hugged the three of them and walked quickly to the door. She gave them a little wave as she stepped out to the walkway that led back to the main building of the resort hotel.

Angie placed her elbow on the arm of the chair and rested her chin in her hand. "Even with all that's going on, I could doze off just sitting here."

Jenna yawned and leaned back on the sofa. "It must be what? Midnight?"

"It's one in the morning. How can you be tired?" Courtney's eyes followed the comings and goings of police officers and technicians. "I know someone died and that's just awful, but it's sort of exciting to watch what's going on here as they try and solve the crime."

Angie closed her eyes. "Maybe you should quit candy-making and join law enforcement."

"Nah. I like making candy. But I'm glad we have some powers and can sometimes help the police."

"Shh." Angie bolted up and spun around looking

to see if anyone had overheard. "Don't talk about that with all these people around. Someone might hear you."

"I'm not dumb, Sis. I don't go around blurting out that I have paranormal powers. Sheesh." Courtney shook her head.

Angie made a face. She glanced over her shoulder to be sure no one was lingering nearby. "Don't say another word."

A heavy sense of gloom wrapped itself around Angie. Although she felt an obligation that they use their powers for good and help the police in any way possible, Angie just wanted to go home, get into her comfortable bed, pull the blanket over her head, and pretend there were no evil-doers in the world.

CHAPTER 6

A young patrolman who the girls had never seen before came into the bungalow. He looked at each girl as if he wasn't expecting to see such young women sitting in the living area of the cottage. "You're the Roselands, right?"

Courtney nodded.

"Chief Martin asked if you'd come along with me. I'll bring you to him."

Courtney was the first one on her feet. "Let's go." Angie and Jenna followed along behind their sister, out of the door, and down the stone pathway to the cottage where the murder took place.

The chief came out. "We're clearing the suite. It'll just be a minute." He gestured for the girls to come inside. "Ellie went home?" He wasn't surprised.

The sisters entered the bungalow with small, slow steps. Some people headed out of the living room and a couple of them took a look at the girls as they passed. Angie could feel tension creeping over her skin and the thrumming started beating in

43

her blood. In times of danger or caution, she and Courtney felt a drum beating in their veins and sometimes, when they were content or at ease, the drum quieted and the beating rhythm turned into a comforting, gentle humming.

"The body is in the bedroom, covered over." The chief tilted his head towards a man wearing a suit standing close to a desk just inside the entrance to the suite. He introduced the sisters to Detective Lang. "He knows about ... your skills. I had to tell him. No need to worry. He knows about such things. He has experience with people who...."

Detective Lang finished the chief's sentence. "People who have powers."

Angie eyed the detective. She didn't like other people knowing about what she and her siblings could do. She didn't want to be judged, and she worried that their abilities would become common knowledge in Sweet Cove, and she definitely did not want that. Perspiration ran down her back.

"Detective Lang and I will stand here, out of the way. The three of you are free to wander about the bungalow. Just don't touch or move anything." The chief and the detective moved quietly to stand near the door.

Angie took a deep breath. She made eye contact with her sisters and they nodded to one another. The girls began to walk around the room each one focusing on something different and moving at their own pace trying to pick up on any shred of evidence or sensation of who had been in the cottage.

Jenna asked, "Where's the gun?"

"It hasn't been found," the chief said. "Yet."

Jenna walked slowly towards the bedroom. She stopped at the threshold and peered in. After several moments, she moved into the room and stood close to the bed. She gazed at the form crumpled under the sheet. She had never met Nelson Rider. She wondered what he looked like. Even though her sisters had described him to her, she wished she had gotten a sense of him when he was alive. Sadness pressed against her chest. She closed her eyes and tried to slow her breathing.

Angie moved about the living room. There was a gas fireplace on the right side wall. She stepped over to it and ran her hand over the marble mantle. Her skin tingled like she was being pricked by a tiny needle. The lights in the room seemed too bright and hurt her eyes. She started to feel light-headed and she gripped the edge of the mantle with her hand and squeezed. Objects in her peripheral vision looked like they were underwater, blurry and washed out.

Angie turned slowly and faced the center of the room. Her ears buzzed and she had the sensation of separating from her body. Her heart beat fast and her throat tightened. Something dark and fleeting like a shadow moved near the bedroom door and was gone.

A scream broke the silence in the room. The sound waves created from the screech sped through the air and pounded Angie's eardrums with such force that it shook her from her trance-like state. Her breath caught in her throat and she shuddered, but within a half second, she was chasing Chief Martin and Detective Lang into the bedroom.

Jenna stood near the bed, white as a ghost. Courtney had reached Jenna first and had her arms around her sister. Angie rushed to Jenna's side and touched her arm.

"What was it?" Chief Martin's face was pale.

Jenna ran her hand over her face. "Did I scream?"

Angie nodded and whispered. "What happened?"

"I was standing here, looking at Nelson's form on the bed. I don't know." Jenna glanced towards the doorway. "Someone was there. I saw the silvery muzzle of the gun." Her eyes went wide. "I heard a shot. The sound was soft though. I thought I heard Nelson scream." She looked at her sisters. "But it wasn't Nelson, was it? It was me? Was I the one who screamed?"

Angie could feel Jenna shaking. Chief Martin gently took the tall brunette by the arm and led her out of the bedroom and into the living room. He sat her down on the sofa and took the seat beside her. "Could you make out who was standing in the doorway?"

46

Jenna thought about what she'd seen and felt. "It was a shadow. I couldn't tell if it was a man or a woman. The figure was dark. The face was shrouded in darkness." Jenna's eyes looked sad. "I'm no help."

Chief Martin squeezed Jenna's shoulder. "You're more help than you know." He looked over at the other two sisters. "Anything?"

Courtney gave a slight shake of her head.

Angie's body was weak like she'd just run ten miles in the heat. Her legs shook. "Before Jenna screamed ... I saw a shadow near the bedroom door." She clasped her arms tight around herself. "Could we get out of here?"

They left the crime scene and stepped outside into the cool, fresh air of the dark night. Angie and Jenna were shaken from the experience in the bungalow. Their shoulders were slumped from a combination of fatigue and anxiety. The chief offered to have an officer give them a lift home and the girls accepted, but they asked if they could be driven back to the Victorian in about thirty minutes. The three sisters wanted to walk around for a while to regain their equilibrium and clear their heads. They decided to wander over to the bluff where their Nana once owned a small cottage and sit in the grass on the point overlooking the ocean.

The girls walked around the lush grounds of the resort in silence and headed to the lawn area on the far side of the property's acreage where they could sit and listen to the waves crashing. Settling on the grass, a slight ocean breeze tickled their skin and the coolness of the salty air was a pleasant contrast to the high heat of the day.

Courtney leaned back on the lawn and looked up at the stars in the black sky. "It's so pretty."

"Who'd imagine the terrible thing that happened a few hours ago on the other side of the hotel building?" Jenna rested in the grass next to Courtney.

"Can you feel the thrumming?" Angie asked.

Courtney smiled. "I always feel it here. It feels good. It feels like home."

Jenna gave a contented sigh. "I don't feel any thrumming, but I feel close to Nana. Calm. Soothing. Like she's near."

Angie could feel the warm humming in her blood that made her feel safe and content. Her muscles relaxed as the anxiety and fear drained away. The rhythmic movement of the ocean waves, rising and falling, breaking against the sand, washed away the tension that had engulfed each girl at the crime scene. The young women rested on the grass, looking up at the stars.

After twenty minutes had passed, Jenna sat up. "I'm feeling better. Want to go home now?"

Angie and Courtney both rose to sitting positions and yawned at the same time, causing them to chuckle.

"Home sounds good." Angie rubbed the back of her neck.

"Remember when Ellie said that dealing with the Winstons wasn't going to be all sweetness and light?" Courtney pushed herself up from the lawn and smiled. "That sister of ours is becoming downright clairvoyant."

CHAPTER 7

Angie yawned as she put a muffin tin into the oven and set the timer. "I'm beat."

"Me, too." Ellie stacked pancakes in the warming tray and returned to the counter to slice fruit. "Even though I got home long before you and the others, I couldn't sleep. I was tossing and turning all night. Jenna's lucky that she doesn't have to be up at the crack of dawn like we do."

Angie smiled slyly. "Maybe I should go wake her."

Tom entered the kitchen. "Did I hear someone say Jenna?" He had his tool belt in his hand.

"She's still asleep. We had a late night last night." Angie started to prepare cookies for an afternoon snack for the B and B guests. She filled Tom in on the goings-on about the latest murder in Sweet Cove. "We were with the police for hours. I only got two hours of sleep."

Tom poured himself some coffee. He sat at the kitchen counter. "What's with all this crime lately? It's never been like this in Sweet Cove. It's usually peaceful and quiet around here."

Ellie brought Tom a plate with blueberry pancakes and bacon. When Euclid and Circe jumped up onto the counter to watch Tom, Ellie scowled at them, but she let them stay.

Tom reached over and gave each cat a cheek scratch. He looked at Angie. "After I eat, how would you like to see the renovations for your bake shop?"

Angie stopped mixing and stared at Tom. Her eyes lit up. "It's ready to show?"

Tom had asked that no one try to get a look at the room that he was renovating for the bake shop so that it would be a surprise when it was ready to be viewed. He even went so far as to tape brown paper on the windows so there would be no peeking.

"There's still quite a lot of finish work left to do, but I think it's time you had a look at it. Now's the time if you want anything changed."

"Eat your breakfast fast." Angie smiled broadly at Tom. "I can't wait to see it."

Mr. Finch entered the kitchen and wished everyone a good morning. Angie told him that Tom was going to unveil the renovations on the bake shop room in a little while. The changes on the Victorian's kitchen and the customer part of the bake shop had been going on for some time. Tom had just about finished the kitchen space, creating a family side and a commercial side. The work was top-notch and it was a pleasure to cook, bake, and gather together in the beautiful new kitchen. In a few weeks, Angie could re-open her Sweet Dreams Bake Shop.

"Are you done eating?" Angie wouldn't refill Tom's coffee until after they got a look at the new room.

"I shouldn't have told you that the room was ready for inspection until after I'd finished my breakfast." Tom grinned. "Let's go. Then I can have another cup of coffee."

Tom, Angie, Ellie, Mr. Finch and the two cats headed for the door that led to the bake shop. Tom opened it in dramatic fashion mimicking the sound of a drum roll. He held his hand out for Angie to enter.

She took a few steps into the room and practically squealed. New windows lined the wall overlooking the wraparound porch and a new door had been installed that led outside. The walls were bead board and would be stained white. The customer counter area had a light gray granite countertop and the work counter against the back wall was made of white marble with swirls of dark and light gray running through it. There were spaces for two refrigerators, the glass case for the goodies, and a separate coffee bar.

Angie nearly swooned. She turned to Tom and bear-hugged him with tears in her eyes. "It's so beautiful. I never imagined such a gorgeous space.

Thank you." She squeezed him.

Ellie and Mr. Finch ran their hands over the lovely new countertops and walked around the room imagining the cafe tables filled with happy customers.

"It's great. It's really beautiful." Ellie smiled at Tom.

"We would expect nothing less from such a superb craftsman. Well done, Tom." Mr. Finch gave a slight bow.

The cats sat on the new counter and trilled.

"I think I did such a good job because I had two taskmasters watching every move I made throughout the process." Tom winked at the cats and then looked at Angie. "They made sure you got your money's worth."

The cats puffed up proudly.

Jenna stumbled into the room from the kitchen wearing pajamas, her hair tousled from sleep. "What's going on?" Her eyes widened when she saw the new bake shop. "Wow. You outdid yourself. It's gorgeous. Maybe I should have you renovate my jewelry room." She gave Tom a hug and a kiss.

Angie smiled. "I can't wait to open the shop." Suddenly remembering she'd put muffins in the oven, she hurried back inside to check that the timer hadn't gone off.

Everyone returned to the kitchen. Assured that the muffins were safe, Angie lifted the coffeepot and rewarded Tom for his hard work by refilling his mug.

Jenna sat at the counter next to Tom. "You heard about last night?" She pushed her uncombed hair back from her face.

Tom nodded. "You and Angie both saw a shadow of what happened?"

"Only slightly," Jenna said. "I saw the shadow of a person and the muzzle of the gun. And I heard a scream, but I think that was me. Then it was gone. It wasn't very helpful."

"Maybe more will come to light?" Tom asked.

"I don't know." Jenna looked at her sisters. "We're so new at this. We don't know how it works or how to control it."

"I think we should talk to Bethany." Ellie placed hard boiled eggs into a bowl. "I'm suspicious of her."

Jenna scrunched her forehead. "Why so?"

"She was here with us when we got the call from Josh to hurry to the resort, but what time did the police say Nelson Rider was killed?"

"Um." Jenna cupped her coffee mug with two hands. "Rider was dead when the housekeeper went into the room around 10:45. Chief Martin said the investigator told him that Nelson Rider died between 10:00 and 10:45pm. Someone saw Rider walking back to his bungalow just after 9:30."

"So," Ellie surmised. "Bethany could have killed Nelson and then rushed here to have an alibi."

54

Angie said, "I didn't think to suspect Bethany, but she could have done it. She didn't arrive here at the Victorian last night until almost eleven. She had plenty of time to shoot Nelson and then high-tail it over here to try to cover up her actions."

"Showing up here so late is kind of suspicious," Tom noted. "And you're right, it could very well be that she came here last night to create an alibi, have people vouch for her whereabouts."

Jenna dipped a piece of pancake into maple syrup. "What about Bethany's friend, Todd Moore? He had motive, too. He might have killed Nelson to get him out of his and Bethany's lives. Eliminate the future husband. Problem solved."

"They might have planned it together." Mr. Finch took a swallow from his tea cup.

"Good thinking." Angie put another tin of muffins into the oven and scooped cookie dough onto a baking sheet.

"Did you know that Senator Winston rented a mansion in Coveside?" Finch added milk to his second cup of tea. "Miss Betty told me. He rented it for a month, to house some of his friends before and after the wedding. The Senator and Bethany were due to check out of the resort today and move to the mansion."

"That's interesting. I wonder if they will change their minds and just leave town now." Ellie carried a tray of pancakes into the dining room for the guests.

"I would think Nelson Rider's brother and sister will sweep into town." Angie placed the cooled muffins into a basket. "They'll probably bring their own private detectives to solve their brother's murder."

"Chief Martin is not going to like the mess that this is going to cause." Tom rinsed his empty mug in the sink. "All kinds of law enforcement will be sticking their hands into the investigation. It will be hard to coordinate all of that."

"I do not envy Chief Martin's position. He has a most difficult job." Mr. Finch toasted an English muffin in the toaster oven and removed raspberry jam from one of the refrigerators.

"I'm off to work on my bake shop masterpiece," Tom kidded. "Call me if you find out anything interesting about the case or you need my help in solving it." He winked and strapped on his tool belt. He gave Jenna a kiss on the cheek. "Come on, cats, enough goofing off. It's time we went to work."

Euclid and Circe jumped down from the top of the fridge and followed Tom into the new bake shop room to supervise his activities.

Jenna looked at Angie. "What do you think? Should we wander down to the inn at the beach and look up Mr. Todd Moore, *friend* of Bethany?"

Angie wiped her hands on a dish towel. "I'd like to know if Bethany was playing us. I'd like to know if she showed up here late last night to cover her tracks. Maybe she wanted to use us as pawns who would vouch for her whereabouts." She loaded some dirty dishes into the dishwasher. "Even though I'd like to stay out of it, I feel like we're in it already. Chief Martin wants our help and I feel obligated to assist him. We need to figure out if Bethany killed her fiancé or not." Angie turned to Jenna and Mr. Finch with serious eyes. "And if she didn't do it, then who did?"

CHAPTER 8

Angie and Jenna headed along Beach Street towards the inns near the beach. "I'll call Josh later today to find out if the Winstons have checked out of the resort. Mr. Finch is going to call Betty and ask if the Senator has contacted her about the house that he's supposed to be renting."

"With the help of our clever contacts, we'll be able to figure out where the Winstons are staying in Sweet Cove or if they've left the area." Jenna looked wistfully out over the ocean as they approached the beach. "Are we ever going to get some time when we can all just relax on the sand like we did at Courtney's birthday party? I feel like the summer is passing us by."

"We need to get everyone together and spend an afternoon at the beach." Angie put her sunglasses on. "And we need to arrange a house-warming party for Mr. Finch."

Jenna said, "His new furniture is being delivered at the end of this week. Let's talk to Ellie and Courtney tonight about a surprise party to celebrate his new home."

Angie eyed the two inns along Beach Street. "Bethany only said that Todd is staying at an inn on the beach. She didn't say which one, so let's start with The Seagull."

"I hope she didn't mean the inns near Coveside. Finding Todd could take a while."

Angie rolled her eyes. "Yeah. Even longer if he's left town."

The girls entered the small lobby of the Seagull Inn and walked up to the desk clerk. Jenna smiled at the man. "We were wondering if you could ring a room for us? We're looking for Todd Moore. A mutual friend told us that he's in town."

The elderly desk clerk smiled at the girls. "Mr. Moore just checked in yesterday." He looked over the girls' heads. "In fact, there he is. He's on the porch." The clerk pointed out the back window to a large covered porch area just off the back door.

The girls thanked the desk clerk and made their way to the porch, thankful that there was only one man sitting outside since they had no idea what Todd looked like.

Angie gave a sigh of relief. "It must be our lucky day."

They stepped out onto the shaded deck. There were café tables and comfortable chairs and lounges to relax on. Several potted palms were placed in the corners of the space. The man sitting at a table with a cold drink glanced up as the girls came out from the lobby.

Jenna smiled. "Todd?"

The man seemed surprised by Jenna's recognition and he looked to be struggling to remember her from somewhere, not realizing that he really didn't know her at all.

Jenna extended her hand. "Jenna Roseland. This is my sister, Angie. We're friends of Bethany."

Angie gestured to the empty chairs around Todd's table. "May we join you?"

Todd nodded. Confusion creased his brow.

The girls sat.

Angie said, "Bethany told us you were in town."

"How do you know Beth?"

"We've just met her recently. We've been helping her arrange her wedding here in Sweet Cove." Angie gave him a friendly look. "She told us you were staying here."

Todd's face clouded, but he didn't say anything. His eyes darted around the deck and garden.

Angie got the feeling he might bolt so she quickly engaged him in conversation. "Bethany speaks highly of you. She told us you've been friends since you were little children."

Jenna leaned slightly forward. "When did you get into town?"

Todd shifted in his chair. "Just recently."

Here we go with evasive answers, Angie thought. She decided that the best thing to do was to stop beating around the bush. "Terrible about Bethany's fiancé."

Todd narrowed his eyes. "What do you mean?"

Jenna's brows furrowed. "Have you seen Bethany since you arrived?" Her tone was careful. "Have you talked to her?"

Todd shook his head. "Not yet." He looked at each girl. "What's wrong with Nelson?"

Angie thought either Todd had no idea what happened to Nelson Rider or that he should be nominated for an Academy Award. "You haven't heard?"

"Heard what?" Todd sat up straighter, clearly becoming alarmed.

Jenna and Angie made eye contact with one another. Jenna kept her voice quiet. "I'm surprised you haven't heard people talking. It's in the newspaper today, on the news. We really shouldn't be the ones to tell you."

Todd's face flushed. His breathing quickened. "Has something happened to Nelson?"

"He ...I'm sorry ... Mr. Rider has passed away." Jenna spoke solemnly.

"What!" Todd jumped up from his chair. "When? What happened?"

"You should talk to Bethany," Angie suggested. "We've only heard bits and pieces." She didn't think they should share all the nasty details with Todd.

"Where is Beth?"

"Um. She was staying at the Sweet Cove Resort

down on Robin's Point." Jenna shrugged. "But we're not sure if she's still there."

Todd headed for the door to the inn. "I need to talk to her. Sorry." He fled into the hotel lobby.

"Well." Angie turned to Jenna. "I'm not sure what I expected, but that wasn't it."

"He sure seemed surprised by the news. It seemed genuine. Why wouldn't Bethany have told him?"

Angie's face was pensive. "Maybe she didn't tell him to keep their contact non-existent. So law enforcement couldn't say they were in on the murder together? Don't call or text each other. Then suspicion isn't raised."

They sat for a few minutes thinking, and then Jenna broke the silence. "Maybe we should find out where Bethany is? I would really like to talk to her, but we probably can't get near her."

Angie pulled out her phone. "I'll text Chief Martin and ask where she is."

"And I'll call Mr. Finch to see if he's talked to Betty yet about whether or not the Winstons are going ahead with their plans to rent the mansion in Coveside."

The girls left the inn's porch deck and headed home. Jenna talked on her phone with Mr. Finch as she walked and Angie waited for a reply text from the chief. She decided to call Josh when she got home to find out how he was faring.

Jenna ended her call. "Mr. Finch says Betty told

him that Senator Winston's assistant picked up the Coveside house key this morning."

"The chief just replied to my text. He confirms that the Winstons have moved to the rental house." Angie looked up from her phone. "There's more privacy at the rental house than at the resort and maybe they don't want to head back to their homes until this mess cools down somewhat. Being in Sweet Cove helps them hide-out from the media."

"That makes sense. I bet the press is dying to swarm them with questions." Jenna made a face. "I wouldn't want the loss of privacy that such a public life would require."

"Having them in Sweet Cove for a while longer will benefit us." Angie pushed her hair back over her ears. "Maybe we can talk to Bethany. Want to take a detour and go to the candy store? I'd like to talk things over with Courtney and Mr. Finch."

The girls passed the Victorian and kept walking up to Main Street where they turned right and headed the couple of blocks past stores and restaurants to the candy shop. The little bell tinkled when they opened the door.

Rufus Fudge stood inside chatting with Courtney. Their eyes were sparkling as the two young people stared at each other.

The girls greeted him. Jenna teased the young Englishman who was interning for the summer at Attorney Jack Ford's office. "Do you actually do any legal work for Attorney Ford? You seem to be more interested in candy."

Fudge's cheeks blushed. "It's my lunch break. I thought I'd come by and get some candy to take back to the office."

Angie leaned closer. "It's okay, Rufus. We know the real reason you like candy so much."

"Leave him alone." Courtney came to the rescue. She gave her sisters gentle nudges. "You two go in the back room. I'll be there in a few minutes."

The twin sisters reluctantly followed Courtney's orders and they shuffled away into the back of the store where Mr. Finch was in the process of making some wonderfully smelling delight.

Angie closed her eyes and inhaled. "What is it?"

"A new flavor of fudge. Miss Courtney and I have been discussing this new flavor and we're giving it a try today." Mr. Finch smiled. "You may be among the first to try it, should things go well."

"I'm happy to just stand here and sniff." Angie chuckled.

Courtney hurried into the work room. Her eyes flashed. "You two need to stop teasing Rufus. It's rude."

Jenna tilted her head. "Really? After all the grief you've given me about Tom?"

"This is different." Courtney put a tray into the sink to wash it out.

"Yes." Jenna crossed her arms. "It's different because now it's *you* getting razzed."

Angie didn't want things to escalate between the

sisters so she changed the subject. "We want to talk over the case with you and Mr. Finch." She brought her youngest sister and Finch up to speed with what they'd discovered about Todd.

"So it seems Todd Moore is in the dark about Nelson's murder?" Courtney sat down in the desk chair. "You thought he was sincere in his shock?"

"It sure seemed like it." Jenna nodded.

"There are a number of things to consider. Perhaps it would be helpful to recap what we know." Mr. Finch poured fudge into a pan. "Nelson Rider has been murdered. Miss Bethany and Todd Moore are in love. Todd has received threats against his life for being in love with Miss Bethany. Senator Winston would not be pleased if he knew the depth of feeling that his daughter has for Todd. Miss Bethany can be considered a suspect in Nelson's murder. Todd appeared not to know what happened, so that probably eliminates him as a suspect. Anything else?" He scraped the pan with a spatula.

"Can I lick the pan?" Angie giggled and stuck a finger into the bottom of the pan Finch was holding. She licked her finger. "Yum. Delicious."

One of the candy store employees stuck her head around the corner to peer into the work room. "Courtney? There's a woman out here who says she needs to see the Roseland sisters. Should I send her back?"

Courtney's face was blank. She looked at her

sisters who appeared to be just as surprised. They shrugged.

Courtney said, "I guess so. Sure. Send her in."

A young woman rushed into the back room. She pulled off her sunglasses and floppy hat. Bethany Winston stood there with wide eyes.

Angie whispered to Mr. Finch. "You know when you asked a few minutes ago if there was anything else to add to the information about the murder case?" She leaned closer. "The answer is 'probably yes.'"

CHAPTER 9

"I had to sneak here." Bethany was breathing hard and she looked back over her shoulder. She stepped further into the room. Her platinum hair was flat and sweaty from being squished under the hat. "I had to slip past the media. They're hanging out near the house we rented." She glanced at the four people staring at her. "Why are you looking at me like that?"

Jenna went over to the woman. "We're just surprised to see you. I'm sorry about Nelson."

The others expressed their condolences. Mr. Finch introduced himself and offered to make Bethany a latte. She accepted and he went to his machine to prepare it.

Courtney gestured to the desk chair and the young woman sat down with a great sigh. "How is this my life?" She plopped her hat and sunglasses on the desk. "Poor, stupid Nelson."

Angie carried two folding chairs over and placed them near the desk. There were two stools next to the wall. Courtney pulled them over. The sisters sat, and Mr. Finch handed the latte to Bethany and then took a chair.

"Why do you say that Nelson was stupid?" Jenna asked.

Bethany ran her hand through her hair and pushed her droopy bangs back off her forehead. "Nelson was the perfect stereotype of a blue-blooded rich boy. He played the part well."

"How do you mean?" Courtney's expression was serious.

"Nelson went to boarding school. He went to Yale. He got into Harvard Business School because his daddy made a call. He was a party boy. His family was always covering for him." She let out a loud sigh. "He only did enough at work to get by. Nelson was always having affairs. Deep down he was a good person, but he just thought life was one big party and he was going to suck up everything he could. Honestly, he was just like a little boy. He never thought his actions would get him into trouble." She shook her head sadly. "It seems he was wrong about that."

"He had affairs while you were engaged?" Jenna made a face.

Bethany waved her hand dismissively. "Of course. He would never stop. There's always a willing Miss, especially if the guy is loaded."

"Why put up with it?" Angie questioned.

"It is what it is." Bethany sipped her latte. "Well, it was what it was." She placed her small white cup on the desk. "I knew what I was getting into by marrying Nelson."

"Why marry someone like that?" Courtney's eyes clouded over. "And when you love someone else?"

Bethany didn't say anything.

Mr. Finch spoke. "Perhaps it was expected of you?"

The platinum blonde gave a sad, little nod. She looked like she'd added ten years to her age since the previous night. "Money, position, power. It's all sooo important," she said wearily.

Angie's heart felt heavy and sorry for Bethany, but then she shook herself, afraid that this might be a performance to throw people off from considering her a suspect. Angie tried tuning in to her senses to pick up on anything the young woman might be giving off, but her thoughts and feelings were muddled. She wished the cats were here.

Courtney asked, "Why did you come to see us?"

"I'm afraid the police will try to pin this on Todd. You know, the love triangle. It's like something out of a terrible movie. I'm worried."

Angie didn't mention that Bethany herself might end up being suspected.

Bethany rubbed her eyes. "I want all of you to look into it. See if you can figure out who killed Nelson."

Courtney leaned over and pulled a pad of paper from the desk drawer. "What can you tell us? Can you think of anyone who might be guilty of the murder?"

"Well, you can start with a few of his recent affairs."

Courtney's eyebrows shot up. "There's more than one right now?"

"Nelson was a busy man. There's one person in particular you should look at though. Nelson had recently broken off with her. Her name is Kim Hutchins. She works at Nelson's family investment firm. She's been Nelson's assistant. I understand that Kim was not very happy to be dumped by Mr. Money Bags."

"She lives in New York?" Jenna asked.

"She works at the Boston office. She lives there in the city."

"What does she look like?" Angie asked even though she had a pretty good idea of what she might look like.

Bethany scowled. "Exactly what you'd expect. Young, blonde, blue eyes, big chest, long legs. Look at the company website, at the staff profiles. She's on there in all her glory."

Jenna stood up and stretched her back muscles. Lack of sleep and too much sitting of late had put a kink in her back. "Is she a financial advisor?"

"She was the office manager until she became Nelson's assistant."

"Can you give us an address for the firm or for Kim's apartment in Boston?" Courtney's pen was poised over the pad of paper.

"You don't have to go to Boston to talk to her."

"Why not?" Angie cocked her head.

"Because, the lovely, Miss Kim Hutchins is right here in Sweet Cove." Bethany's lips turned down. "I saw her in town the other day."

"Well, isn't that convenient." Mr. Finch looked over the top of his glasses, one gray eyebrow raised in suspicion.

Bethany's phone tweeted in her purse and she pulled it out. She checked the screen, and shoved it back into the pocket of her bag without answering. "It's my father. I'm surprised he doesn't put one of those prison ankle GPS things on me so he can track me wherever I go." She stood up. "I'd better get back before he puts out an all points bulletin." Bethany reached for her hat and glasses. "Oh, I almost forgot to mention. We're having a remembrance gathering for Nelson at the house we've rented. It will be more private there. It will be easier to keep the media at bay." She pulled a piece of paper from her purse and handed it to Angie. "Would you be able to provide the desserts?" Without waiting for the answer, Bethany looked at Courtney and Mr. Finch. "And would you be able to make some candy items for after the service? It's all listed there on the paper, the things we want. The date and time are written at the top." She blew out a long sigh. "I'd like you all to be present, as well. Wander around, talk to the attendees, and see if you can flesh out some information. I wouldn't be surprised if any one of the guests is the killer. Most of them are vipers in one way or another."

Angie glanced at the list of treats that the Winstons were requesting. "Okay. We can provide the sweets." She made eye contact with Bethany. "Jenna and I ran into Todd earlier today."

Bethany's eyes narrowed. "Ran into...?"

"We sought him out." Jenna admitted. "He claimed not to know anything about what happened to Nelson. You should call him."

"You told him?" Bethany made a sour face.

"He was going to hear it anyway. It's all over town, it's on the news." Angie stood up. "I was surprised he hadn't heard from you."

"It was better that Todd didn't know what happened."

"Why?" Angie pressed. If she was going to investigate the case, she wanted Bethany to be forthcoming.

"Todd gets upset easily." Bethany headed for the front room. "I have to go. I'll be in touch." She walked briskly away and was gone.

The three sisters and Mr. Finch exchanged looks.

"What do you think?" Courtney asked.

Angie moved to the preparation counter. "I think I need a piece of fudge."

"Todd gets upset easily?" Jenna frowned. "That was a strange statement. A murder is something to get upset over. It would be within the boundaries of normal behavior for someone to get upset when a person is murdered."

Mr. Finch cut some squares from one of the pans of fudge. He placed a piece on a napkin and handed it to Angie. She took a bite of the creamy square and closed her eyes in delight. "Wonderful." She took another bite and gave a little grin. "I needed that. Bethany gives me low blood sugar."

Mr. Finch's eyes twinkled. "Perhaps Miss Bethany gives her friend, Todd, low blood sugar as well, and then he becomes more vulnerable to upset."

Courtney shook her head and smiled at Mr. Finch's comment. She headed to the sink to finish washing the trays. "It's a good thing we each have a sense of humor. Otherwise...."

"So what's next, besides the remembrance service?" Jenna moved to the counter and made herself a latte. "We hunt down Kim Hutchins and interview her about her affair with Nelson?"

"Yes." Angie nodded. "But maybe we do it without just blurting out that we know about the affair."

"A bit of finesse would be useful during the questioning." Mr. Finch checked the new batch of fudge.

"How do we find her?" Courtney asked.

"I guess we'll have to call around to the inns and hotels and ask for her." Angie did not relish the

73

idea of calling all of the overnight establishments in Sweet Cove trying to find out where Ms. Hutchins was staying.

Courtney dried the candy trays. "I wish there was some way to bring the cats to the memorial gathering."

They all looked at each other.

"That will take some thought." Angie considered.

"But, it is certainly not out of the realm of possibility." Mr. Finch finished cutting the tray of fudge into squares, a sly smile on his lips. "I might have an idea."

It seemed that two fine felines just might end up paying their respects at the Winston's planned remembrance service for Mr. Nelson Rider.

CHAPTER 10

After leaving Courtney and Finch at the candy store, Angie and Jenna walked down Beach Street towards the Victorian and as they approached they noticed a young woman sitting in a rocker on the porch holding a mug.

Jenna squinted. "Who's that?"

"Must be a new B and B guest."

Angie and Jenna turned onto the walkway that led to the porch. The woman gave them a big smile. "Afternoon."

The girls returned the greeting. As Angie opened the door to the house, her heart thudded and she stopped so suddenly on the threshold that her sister almost slammed into her back. Jenna looked over Angie's shoulder wondering why she had halted. "What? Why'd you stop?"

Angie wanted to return to the porch, but decided it would appear awkward, so she continued into the foyer. Once Jenna was inside too, her sister whirled around and whispered. "On the porch. That girl is blonde. She has a big chest."

Jenna narrowed her eyes, trying to understand why Angie was making those observations when she suddenly knew the answer. "Is it the girl who had an affair with Nelson Rider?"

The door opened and the attractive blonde entered. Her face lost its smile when she saw the two sisters standing in the foyer whispering. The girls turned slowly with stupid grins on their faces hoping the blonde hadn't heard their conversation.

"Hi again." Angie stuck out her hand and introduced herself. "This is Jenna. Our sister, Ellie, runs the guest inn."

The blonde seemed slightly wary, but she shook hands. "Nice to meet you." She went into the dining room to check out the afternoon snacks.

Jenna made eye contact with her sister and Angie shrugged. Ellie came into the room carrying a small tray of cookies. "Oh, you're back. What did you find out?"

"We're going to the kitchen to get something to eat." Angie forced a smile and nodded towards the back of the house. "Come see us when you're free."

A few minutes later, Ellie met her sisters in the kitchen. "Why are you acting so weird?"

"Who's the blonde?" Jenna questioned.

"A new guest." Ellie put her hands on her hips.

"What's her name?" Angie was growing impatient.

"Kimberley Hutchins."

Jenna and Angie high-fived each another while

76

Ellie made a face.

"She made it easy for us." Jenna grinned.

"What do you mean?" Ellie wanted to know what was going on.

"We ran into Bethany." Angie kept her voice soft. "She told us that our new guest, Miss Hutchins, was having an affair with Nelson." She paused for effect. "And that Nelson recently broke it off with her, probably to move on to someone else."

Ellie's eyebrows shot up. "Nelson Rider was having an affair right before he was getting married?" She gave a grave shake of her head. "Bah. That's shameful. What was wrong with him?" She went to the refrigerator and poured herself a glass of juice.

"We heard a bunch of other stuff about Nelson." Jenna took a sip from Ellie's glass while her sister was returning the juice bottle to the fridge. "We'll fill you in later. We need to talk to the new guest."

Ellie had moved to the sink and was glancing out the window into the backyard as she ran water over some plates to rinse them. She pointed towards the back of the house. "Kimberley's outside, sitting in the garden."

Jenna and Angie went out the back door. They thought it might be helpful to go sit in the fresh air for a little while. Angie looked around for the cats, but they were nowhere to be seen. Stepping into the yard, the girls spotted the young woman sitting under the pergola surrounded by flowers and shrubs.

"Oh, hi there." Angie approached. "Mind if we sit with you?" She sat down in the chaise opposite Kimberley Hutchins.

Jenna sat next to Angie. She leaned back in the chair and closed her eyes. "What a beautiful day."

"It's perfect." Kimberley agreed.

"What brings you to Sweet Cove?" Angie hoped to start a conversation.

"Well, it started out as a mini-vacation. A friend and I planned to meet, but she had to cancel. I decided to come up anyway."

"Where are you from?"

"Boston."

Angie continued the conversation with the young woman, telling her that she and her sisters had grown up in Boston and had moved to Sweet Cove only recently to start businesses. Kimberley said that she was raised in central Massachusetts and moved to Boston for a job. That bit of information gave Angie an opening to ask what she did for work.

"I'm an assistant to a vice president at a large financial institution." Kimberley's long dark lashes flitted over her eyes. She had two dimples in her rosy cheeks. The young woman was sweetly beautiful, not heavily made-up or self-conscious about her good looks.

Angie thought that Kimberley was someone who should be in a shampoo or a skin care commercial and that whatever it was she advertised, Angie was sure she would be convinced to buy the products. "What's the name of the firm?"

Kimberley said, "Rider Financial."

Angie feigned surprise. "The man who was murdered in Sweet Cove the other day ... isn't that the company he worked for? His name was Nelson Rider. Did you know him?"

Kimberley fidgeted in her seat. Her eyes flashed for a second as she pushed her hair behind her ear. "Yes, I did."

Jenna and Angie offered condolences.

"That's awful." Jenna's face was lined with concern. "Did you know him well?"

"Well enough." Kimberley looked out over the garden. For a moment, the muscles of her face seemed to tremble and her eyes looked moist. "I'll be attending his memorial. It's being held here in town. That's why I've extended my stay."

"I wonder what happened. Why would someone kill him?" Angie eyed the young woman hoping she might go on with the discussion. "Who would want him dead?"

Kimberley swallowed hard and then gave a little snort. "Probably a whole lot of people." She picked at her fingernail. "He was a wealthy man in a cut-throat business, but members of his family were the brains behind the organization. Nelson wasn't your typical high-achieving financier. He liked to play. A lot."

"Did his family resent his behavior?" Jenna asked.

"People have different opinions on that." Kimberley pushed her long blonde hair over her shoulder.

Angie leaned forward. "What do *you* think?"

"I think Nelson did things that made people angry. He wasn't serious about his work." Kimberley looked around the yard. "He messed up pretty badly on something important not long ago."

"A business deal?" Jenna looked intrigued.

The blonde woman nodded. "It was worth millions. His brother, Geoffrey, is a president at the family firm. He was livid. I thought he would fire Nelson, but he let him off the hook again. When I first heard that Nelson was dead, you know what my first reaction was? That maybe he did himself in because of his mess-up." She gave a little chuckle. "But then I realized that he would never do such a thing. Nelson loved his life."

"Who do you think killed him? Do you have any thoughts?" Angie made eye contact with Kimberley. "Since you work in the office, you must hear a lot of stuff that's going on."

Kimberley blew out a long breath. "I hear plenty. More than I want to know. In fact, I've given my notice. I've had enough of that family's antics." She stood up. "I'm going up to my room to take a nap. Nice talking with you." She walked through the backyard, up the stairs to the wraparound porch, and headed to the front door of the Victorian.

Jenna shifted to look at her sister. "She showed some emotion when we talked about Nelson's murder, but she didn't seem to be in love with him. I didn't see the depth of emotion you would expect in a lover, no deep look of sorrow or loss."

"It's more like she's angry with him. Maybe her love and affection changed to disgust or fury when he broke it off with her."

"Do you get the sense that she really did have an affair with Nelson? Do you get the feeling that she might have killed him?"

Angie looked at the flower garden, her mind working. "I don't know. I'm not sure what to think. There are a number of people we could suspect. Kimberley might not have had an affair at all. That could just be Bethany either trying to throw us off or maybe not really knowing who Nelson had affairs with."

Ellie came out of the back door of the house carrying a tray with three glasses of lemonade and a plate of cookies. She placed the tray on the outdoor side table next to where her sisters were sitting. "I brought cold drinks and a snack."

"I love you," Jenna teased.

Ellie ignored the comment and passed Jenna one of the glasses of ice cold lemonade. She settled in the chair that Kimberley had vacated. "So, how did it go? What did you learn?"

"Not a whole lot." Angie sipped her drink and then proceeded to share with Ellie what they found out from the B and B guest. "Have the cats met Kimberley?"

"They did." Ellie stretched out on the chaise. "Gee, it feels good to sit for a minute. The cats were not friendly when they met Kimberley, but they didn't hiss or arch their backs when they saw her. They kept their distance though." She ran her finger along the condensation on her glass. "You know, I think they are becoming wary of people. Remember how they didn't seem to like Charlie Cook or Brian Hudson, but it was never completely clear if they suspected either of them of wrongdoing." Cook and Hudson were both involved in the most recent crime that the Roseland sisters investigated.

"Why do you think that happened?" Jenna had her eyes closed again.

Angie spoke up. "I was thinking about that recently. I wonder if the cats got confused because Charlie had a difficult life, his parents ignored him, sent him away to school. He didn't seem to be loved. And Brian, well, his father abused him and Cook threatened him. Maybe the cats had a hard time sorting out the negative stuff that the two men had suffered from the bad that one of them inflicted on others."

"That makes a lot of sense." Ellie nodded. "Like there's too much static to hear what's really going on."

"Could this be the same thing this time?" Jenna sat up and reached for a cookie. "The cats sense something is off, but there is some competing influence that blocks the clarity of the signal."

"I think that happens with us too." Angie shielded her eyes from the sun. "Sometimes, it's hard to cut through to what I'm really sensing. I feel the thrumming, but I'm not sure what it's trying to tell me. I feel a lot of static involved in this case."

"We need to be careful. Listen and watch, but question everything we hear and see. Try to sift through the static that's blocking what we sense." Jenna's face was serious. "We need to protect ourselves. We've had some close calls in the past month."

Ellie went quiet. Just as the girls turned to see why she'd stopped commenting, they saw her eyes darken. "Someone's coming." Her voice was ominous.

CHAPTER 11

Angie and Jenna sat up in their seats, alarmed. They flicked their eyes towards the house and then turned back to Ellie, their faces questioning.

"What is it?" Angie whispered. "Who's coming?"

A slow smile played over Ellie's lips. "It's just Mr. Finch." She tilted her head to the property line. The older man emerged from the trees that grew between their two back yards. "Did you think I'd had a premonition?" Ellie joked with her sisters.

Jenna gave Ellie a gentle bop on the arm. "You tricked us."

Angie scowled. "I thought something bad was about to happen." She waved at Mr. Finch who was leaning on his cane and making his way to the pergola. When he reached the patio, Angie said, "Ellie played a trick on us. She said someone was coming, like she'd had a vision of something bad."

Finch grinned. "How amusing." He lowered himself onto one of the Adirondack chairs. "Where are the cats?" He glanced around.

Angie narrowed her eyes. "Why?"

"I enjoy their company, is all, Miss Angie. No need to be concerned." Finch gestured to the trees at the back of the property. "I'm going to get some estimates from two stonemasons about putting in that walkway between our houses. I get caught on the branches and roots and nearly fall every time I come through the brush."

"Call us when you're on your way over here and one of us will meet you," Ellie suggested.

"We can't have you hurt." Angie gave him a wink. "We need you to help us solve crimes."

The girls told Finch that Kimberley Hutchins had just checked in at the B and B. They relayed what she'd said about Nelson Rider and his recent costly mistake at the firm.

"Could someone from the firm be responsible for Nelson's death?" Finch placed his cane on the ground next to his chair. "Someone who was tired of his mistakes? Nelson's error cost the firm a great deal of money. Money is a common reason for murder."

"Have you been watching murder mysteries with Courtney?" Angie grinned.

"No. Well, sometimes I do, but I read this information in a newspaper article not long ago. It makes a good deal of sense." Finch stroked his chin. "Money is a powerful motivator. For good and evil."

"What should we do next?" Jenna asked. "Who

should we talk to? Is there anything else we can do besides interview people?"

Angie's expression turned serious. "Josh told me that the bungalow where Nelson was killed is going to be closed all summer and then in the fall they're going to knock it down."

"That's probably wise." Finch considered.

"Police Chief Martin would like us to go through the place again." Angie paused and looked at Mr. Finch. "I was thinking that maybe you should come and visit the bungalow with us. Walk around, touch things. Maybe you'll pick up on something in the rooms."

Finch nodded. "I'd be happy to accompany you to the cottage if you think it might be useful."

"Also, we should bring the cats along," Ellie said. "It might help them clarify their feelings about people and then that would help us know who we can trust."

"And who *not* to trust, which might be even more helpful." Jenna shrugged a shoulder. "When can we go?"

"Courtney should come too." Angie thought that with all of them working on finding clues and trying to sense something, they would be more successful with everyone together. "At dinner, let's figure out when we're all free to make a visit to the resort. And we should talk about the upcoming memorial service too."

Ellie eyed Mr. Finch. "You said you had an idea

for bringing the cats to the remembrance service?"

Finch had a gleam in his eye. "The cats could attend as therapy animals. They would be present to help calm and comfort people. I saw this very thing when I was living in Chicago."

"Euclid would hate that." Jenna thought about the big orange cat being pawed by strangers.

"We could explain the mission to him and appeal to his better nature." Mr. Finch looked at one of the windows at the back of the Victorian and spotted Euclid sitting on the windowsill staring out at them. "Oh, look. There he is now. He probably heard us talking about him." Finch waved.

"And at this very minute, Euclid is sitting there coming up with excuses to avoid the memorial event." Jenna leaned back against the sun-warmed wood of the chair.

Mr. Finch smiled. "He *is* a very clever boy."

***

At dinner the group discussed arranging a time to re-visit the crime scene bungalow at the resort. After everyone had confirmed when they were free, and Police Chief Martin was consulted, they decided to meet at the bungalow at the end of the week.

When everything was settled, Jenna suggested that the four of them head to the beach for a quick swim in the ocean before Courtney needed to return to the candy shop for the evening shift. Mr. Finch was invited to the beach as well, but he had a date with Betty, the Sweet Cove Realtor and his girlfriend of two months.

The sisters headed down Beach Street to the white sand beach. The crowds of the day had left for dinner, but there were still plenty of people lingering by the sea. The girls loved to be on the beach at this time of day as the setting sun painted rosy streaks of pink and violet across the sky.

They brought boogie boards with them to ride the waves. Once they pulled off their T-shirts and shorts and tossed them on the sand alongside their beach towels, the four girls raced each other into the water. The sisters jumped the waves and dove under them as they crested. The tide was going out and as it slowly retreated, the beach grew wider.

The sea swung around the back of the beach and created a saltwater river where people kayaked and floated in inner tubes. The girls headed to the river with their boards and walked upstream where they stepped into the water and floated along with the current until it carried them back to the main beach. The girls stood up out of the water with their boards and headed back to where they started so they could float down a second time.

"It's great this evening." Courtney said to her sisters. "The water is warmer than usual and the air temperature is perfect." Stepping into the water and leaning on her board, she started kicking vigorously. "Race you to the end of the river." She took off downstream.

Jenna kicked and floated along in hot pursuit of her youngest sister. Angie and Ellie's boards crashed into each other causing Ellie to capsize. Laughter rose into the air as Ellie surfaced and maneuvered back onto her board. Despite the furious fluttering of her legs, she couldn't catch up to the other three.

At the river's end, the four girls beached themselves and sat on the sand for a few minutes.

Courtney leaned back and stretched out on the soft, white sand. "That was so much fun. I don't want to go back to the candy store tonight. I want to stay and do another river run."

"Me, too, but we should head home." Jenna brushed sand from her legs. "I need to get busy on some jewelry. I've been so distracted by things lately and I really have to finish some product to ship out."

Ellie blew out a breath. "No wonder you've been distracted. First, we get hired for a wedding by those crazy Winstons, then the groom is murdered, and now the Winstons contract with all of you to cater desserts and sweets for the memorial reception. Not to mention all of us being asked to investigate Nelson Rider's murder. It's been a nutty few days with a nutty group of people."

Angie sighed. "And we don't have any strong leads on the killer either."

The girls stood up, gathered their things and walked towards Beach Street. They started to discuss the surprise house-warming gathering that they were planning for Mr. Finch when Jenna pulled on Angie's arm and whispered. "Look up there. On the second floor terrace. Isn't that Kimberley Hutchins talking to Todd Moore?" She steered her sisters into a crowd of people standing in line on the sidewalk waiting for entry into a popular restaurant.

Ellie squinted and craned her neck to see.

"Don't be so obvious," Jenna scolded. "It's Bethany's *friend*." She emphasized the word. "That's Todd Moore up there."

"Well, that's definitely Kimberley with him." Ellie stood peering over the shoulder of a tall man who was standing in the line. She was hidden from view, but could clearly see the two people engrossed in conversation on the restaurant's second floor balcony.

Courtney watched them. "How would they know each other?"

The attractive blonde was gesturing in an animated way. She was not smiling. Todd shook his head in response to what Kimberley was telling him.

"And," Angie asked, "What on earth are they discussing? It sure looks like a serious conversation. I wish we could hear what they're saying to each other."

Todd and Kim seemed about to part. Courtney pulled on Angie's arm. "Don't let them see us." The four girls hurried under the restaurant awning.

Courtney narrowed her eyes. "Why are those two talking? Todd is supposed to be in love with Bethany and Kim was having an affair with Bethany's fiancé. Kim would be Bethany's enemy so how does it make any sense that Todd would meet up with Kim to have a chat?"

"Could they have joined forces to kill Nelson Rider?" Ellie watched for the two people to emerge from the restaurant. "Nelson dumped Kim, and a dead Nelson would be a benefit to Todd. Maybe Kim and Todd decided to work together to eliminate a common enemy."

"This is getting more complicated by the minute." Angie slunk down behind a group of people. "Maybe we should split up. Go home in pairs. That way we can blend in with the tourists easier."

Jenna handed Ellie a hair tie. "Pull your hair up into a topknot. That long blonde hair of yours is like a shining beacon. Let's be as inconspicuous as possible." Once Ellie secured her hair, she and Jenna moved through the crowd with their heads down, walking away up Beach Street towards the Victorian.

"Let's wait a minute, and then we'll follow." Keeping an eye on the entrance to the restaurant, Angie saw Todd exit through the front door. "There he goes."

"Should I follow him? He's never met me, so he won't be suspicious." Courtney kept her eyes on Todd as he dodged around the tourists.

"Okay, yeah, go ahead. I'll wait for Kimberley to come out and I'll see where she goes. Text me. Let me know what's going on."

Courtney slid around the people on the sidewalk and hung back from Todd just far enough behind to be of no notice, but close enough to keep him in view. Just as Angie turned her head to watch the restaurant door, Kimberley sauntered out wearing tight black slim leg jeans and a skimpy top that caught the eye of just about every man waiting in the line. Oblivious to any attention, the curvy blonde headed away from the beach area and up the street towards the center of Sweet Cove. On the spur of the moment, Angie decided to catch up to the young woman and try to engage her in conversation, so she darted onto the sidewalk and hurried to Kimberley's side. Angie called out a greeting.

Kimberley whirled towards the voice, her jaw set and her eyes flashing with annoyance. "Oh. It's you."

Not exactly a pleasant hello, but Angie decided it was better than being ignored. "I thought it was you." Angie forced a cheerful tone. "I saw you come out of the restaurant. Are you heading back to the B and B?"

Kimberley's expression remained stern. "What? Yeah."

"Did you meet friends for dinner?" Angie clutched her boogie board and beach towel under her arm. Her wet bathing suit was making her feel cold.

"You ask a lot of questions."

"My sisters always say that." Angie tried to remain friendly in order to stimulate some conversation. "I took a quick swim. I've been working too much and needed a break."

Kimberley said nothing.

"Are you enjoying your stay in Sweet Cove?"

"Not really." The blonde kept her eyes looking forward. She picked up her pace, eager to get away from the pesky interrogator.

Since she was getting nowhere by being pleasant, Angie decided to change her approach. "Funny. When I was coming up from the beach, I thought I saw you on the balcony of the restaurant talking to Todd Moore."

Kimberley whirled around. Her eyes bore into Angie's like lasers. She took a menacing step that closed the space between the two young women. "I don't know what you think you saw." Kim's voice was like ice. "But maybe you'd better get your eyes examined." She held Angie's gaze for several seconds before turning on her heel and storming away.

A chill ran down Angie's spine and it wasn't

because she was wearing a cold, wet swimsuit.

CHAPTER 12

A security guard held up his hand to have Ellie come to a stop in front of a barrier that blocked the entrance to the driveway. She leaned out of the van window. "We're here to attend the memorial. We're also catering the desserts for the event."

A flock of reporters and photographers stood together across the street from the entrance to the home. Several police officers were present to control the media and to help direct traffic.

The security guard peered into the van. His eyebrows went up when he saw the two cats perched next to Mr. Finch in the vehicle's second row seats. "You're bringing cats to a memorial service?" He looked skeptically at Ellie.

She cleared her throat. "In fact, these are therapy animals." Ellie narrowed her eyes. "You *have* heard of therapy animals and the great good they offer to grieving people?"

"Do you have an invitation?" The guard wasn't going to be drawn into conversation.

In the front passenger seat, Angie rustled

through her purse and withdrew the card they'd received from Bethany Winston. She passed it to Ellie, who handed it to the guard. "My sisters are in the station wagon behind us. They are included in this invitation."

After staring at the engraved card and turning it over several times, the security guard handed it back to Ellie with a shrug. "Okay." He waved at the two young men who were manning the barrier and they swung the gate-like structure open to admit the van and the station wagon.

Ellie pressed on the gas pedal. "What an annoying man."

"He's just keeping out the uninvited." Angie watched the landscape rush by as they made their way down the long driveway passing fields, mature trees, and stone walls. As their vehicle approached the house, an attendant indicated where they should park and Jenna pulled her car up beside Ellie's van. Everyone piled out of the vehicles. Euclid jumped from the backseat and sauntered a few feet towards the front entrance of the massive contemporary mansion.

"Wait for us." Jenna warned the orange cat. There were so many cars pulling in for the reception and people approaching the house that Jenna worried something might happen to Euclid and she wanted him to stay close. Euclid sat down next to Circe and they waited for the others.

Before they'd left the Victorian, Euclid had been

completely indignant when Angie tried to stuff him into a cat carrier and he put up such a fuss that they abandoned the idea. "No one is going to believe that you're a normal cat if you don't show up in a carrier."

Euclid glared at Angie and licked his ruffled fur before raising his orange plume of a tail high in the air and strolling out of the house and into the van.

"At least he's agreed to go to the memorial." Mr. Finch had attempted to assure Angie that things would go smoothly once they arrived at the remembrance. Angie just shook her head.

The four sisters removed trays and boxes of desserts and candy from the rear of Jenna's station wagon. Staff from the Winston's rental house hurried out to carry the treats inside. When everything had been delivered, the sisters, Mr. Finch, and the two cats walked along the stone sidewalk to the front entrance of the cream-colored architectural beauty.

"I've never seen this place." Courtney's eyes were like saucers. "You can just see a bit of the roof when you stand on Robin's Point."

"I knew it was some huge place." Ellie glanced around at the perfect landscaping. "But I never expected it was like this."

Decks jutted out from the side of the building overlooking the ocean and expansive lawns edged with flower gardens reached towards the rocky coast. Waves crashed against the shore and the cry of a gull could be heard high overhead.

At the front door, a man in a suit eyed the cats, but didn't mention them as he greeted the girls and Mr. Finch and gestured for them to enter through the massive foyer where they would join the crowd gathered in the two story living room. Two walls were floor-to-ceiling glass and afforded a spectacular view out over the sea. People stood in small groups, chatting quietly, sometimes a sniffle or some weeping mingled in with the talking. The occasional chuckle was heard, but whoever let it slip out realized the error right away and returned to a somber demeanor.

Bethany Winston, dressed in a black sleeveless sheath dress, stood near the windows with several men and women and when she spotted the Roseland sisters, she excused herself and hurried over. Mr. Finch and the girls once again offered condolences.

"Welcome to the snake pit." The rims of Bethany's eyes were red.

"Is there someone here you consider a friend?" Jenna glanced around the room at the crowd wondering if there was someone present that Bethany felt comfortable with.

"Mostly acquaintances." Bethany folded her arms over her chest. "My best friend is in Africa. I told her not to bother coming all this way." She lowered her voice and looked behind her. "Todd is here, of course, but we can only mingle together with our mutual friends."

The girls had decided not to mention to Bethany that they'd seen Todd and Kimberley Hutchins chatting heatedly together at the restaurant near the beach. Courtney followed Todd that night, but he'd only walked back to the inn where he was staying, so there was nothing to report on that front. The sisters were wary about Kimberley's intimidating behavior towards Angie and automatically moved her to the top of the suspect list.

"Is Kimberley here?" Angie's voice shook a little.

"She sure is. Although I must say she looks quite understated this afternoon. I haven't spoken to her. I just glare whenever she comes near. I think she gets the message." Bethany breathed out a long sigh. "I'm ready to drop. These past few days, all of these people treating me like I've lost the love of my life. It's exhausting to play the part of the grieving fiancé and pretend that Nelson was such a virtuous, dedicated partner."

"Is Nelson's family here?" Ellie looked about the room.

"He only has his older brother and sister." Bethany pointed them out on the far side of the room. The sister, a short, slender, well-dressed woman in her mid-forties, her pale blonde hair cut into a bob, was dabbing at her eyes with a tissue. An older woman was consoling the blonde.

In contrast to the grieving sister, the brother

appeared to be holding court in front of a small group of people. Geoffrey looked like an older version of Nelson, tall, fit, well-groomed, nothing out of place, and with a blinding smile. He had an added air of entitlement about him and a quietly simmering power seemed to emanate from his eyes.

Bethany continued, "In some ways I think they feel as I do. Nelson was a thorn in their sides, always goofing off, making mistakes, getting into trouble. They were always bailing him out. I think the brother is particularly pleased that he could be the top dog now with only his sister to challenge him." Bethany scoffed. "Though Nelson would never have been able to challenge Geoffrey or Georgia for control of the company. They are both workaholics and highly intelligent businesspeople."

The girls eyed each other wondering if the brother might be a suspect.

"The brother doesn't seem to be grieving." Courtney asked.

Bethany turned to Courtney, an expression of alarm on her face. "You don't suspect him, do you?"

"Why not?" Courtney watched the man speaking intently with someone in the group.

Bethany gave a slight shake of her head. "I … well. I can't see him as the murderer, but well, I guess he could have set it up." She narrowed her eyes. "I hadn't considered him a suspect. I really don't think that's plausible."

Geoffrey spotted Bethany from across the room and headed over. Introductions were made.

"Are you okay?" Geoffrey put his hand on the small of Bethany's back. She stiffened and gave a slight nod.

The sisters and Mr. Finch offered expressions of sympathy to the brother.

Geoffrey shook his head. "Nelson. Such a free spirit. If only he had applied himself sooner, and not been so trusting of others."

"You think his trust in others is what got him into trouble?" Angie wondered what the brother meant. Something about Geoffrey picked at her skin. She wanted to move away from him.

"I'm sure you heard that Nelson liked to play. Sometimes there are unsavory characters who want to party with a wealthy man. Nelson may have run into a few."

"Did Nelson associate with people like that?" Jenna questioned.

"Let's say that they tried to associate with him." Geoffrey put his hand in the pocket of his suit jacket. "If only Nelson had lived to enact our plan. We were quite sure he would have finally found an avenue for success."

Ellie tilted her head. "Plan?"

"Bethany didn't tell you? We were backing Nelson in a run for the Senate representing our home-state. He was going to announce two weeks after the marriage. We thought it was an excellent career move for Nelson." Geoffrey said to Bethany, "It's nearly time to go in."

"I'll be along in a minute." Bethany turned slightly away from him.

Geoffrey gave everyone a dismissive nod and moved to other side of the room.

Angie said, "So Nelson was going to run for the Senate?"

Bethany gave a loud sigh. "That is the reason for the wedding rush. Wouldn't it look wonderful to the voters? Nelson, from a respected family, a newly married man with a lovely successful wife, who just happens to be the daughter of a former Senator, the popular Norman Winston." She rolled her eyes. "Geoffrey, Georgia, and my father thought that a run for office would be the thing to get Nelson on track. And," she paused, "Nelson was a pushover. They planned to control Nelson to their whims, have him vote in the Senate according to their wishes. Geoffrey was thrilled with the idea. Send Nelson to Washington, get him out of the company."

"Did Nelson want to be a Senator?" Courtney asked.

Bethany snorted. "No. He was happy with his life the way it was. He played and partied. Being an elected official would have put a crimp in his lifestyle." She gave Courtney a look. "I know what your next question is going to be. Then why was Nelson going to run? Because that is what was expected of him. Nelson's and my lives were planned out by others. No one asked our opinion. We do what we're supposed to do." Bethany noticed the family gathering by the windows. "I need to join the others."

"Before you do, tell us how today is going to go." Angie wanted to know how they should proceed at the event.

"There will be a brief remembrance service. A pastor from Nelson's church is here. We'll all move into the next room where seats are set up. The pastor will lead some prayers and then Nelson's friend will speak, followed by a work colleague. Then we'll have the reception. Cremation and burial have taken place already."

"So you want us to mingle around during the reception?" Courtney saw that people were already moving towards the next room.

"Talk to people. If they ask, say you knew me in college. Listen to conversations." Bethany shook her head. "Look at all these people, most are powerful and wealthy beyond imagining, leaders of the business world. Any one of them could be a suspect." She gave a slight snort. "If a bomb went off in here, the world economy would collapse."

When she heard the word 'bomb,' Ellie's eyes widened in horror and her hand flew up to her mouth.

Courtney noticed Ellie's reaction and, in an attempt to relieve her sister's worry, she whispered in mock seriousness. "I didn't realize that you cared about the economy."

Ellie glared and Mr. Finch suppressed a smile at Courtney's comment.

A woman gestured for Bethany to come forward with the family and enter the room where the memorial would take place. As she stepped forward, Bethany noticed something near the window. Euclid and Circe sat on a side table watching the guests. "How did cats get in here?"

"Oh, we brought them." The cats shifted their focus to the Roseland sisters and Courtney smiled at them. "They're very good at solving crimes."

Bethany gave Courtney a look mixed with worry and disbelief.

Mr. Finch twirled his cane on the gleaming wood floor. "Miss Courtney is a jokester. The cats are therapy animals."

Bethany moved away, her eyes narrowed into slits. She muttered to herself. "How is this my life?"

"Must you always comment about the cats being able to solve crimes?" Ellie nervously smoothed her skirt and frowned at Courtney. "People don't realize you're joking."

Courtney shrugged. "That's because I'm *not* joking." Her eyes twinkled as she winked at the cats. She led her family to the next room, falling in behind the long line of attendees filing in for the memorial.

CHAPTER 13

Immediately following the service, the guests were directed through the living room and into a massive dining area where a buffet had been set up with hot and cold food items. The tables groaned with the choices of salads, casseroles, grilled vegetables, baked chicken breasts, filet mignon, breaded fish, and vegetarian options. Wait staff moved about the rooms carrying platters of appetizers and trays with flutes of champagne and glasses of wine. A string quartet played classical music in a corner of the living space.

The earlier somber tone that had kept the guests subdued prior to and during the memorial service had been replaced with a lively energy as people chatted, drank, and ate. The dining and living rooms' doors were now flung open and people, with their food and drink, spilled out onto the terraces and decks.

Mr. Finch and the girls noticed that the cats were perched on a table near the open doors and were being cooed over and patted by some of the guests. Euclid didn't seem to mind the attention.

"I'm planning on teasing Euclid when we get home." Courtney nodded at the cats. "He put up such a stink about coming here and, now, look at him. He's like a king holding court with his subjects."

"I hope he and Circe run into some of our suspected killers so that we can gauge their reactions to them." Jenna scanned the room looking for Bethany, Todd, or Kimberley.

"I guess the best thing to do would be to split up and spread out among the people." Angie nervously pushed her hair behind her ear. She looked about for Kimberley and hoped to avoid her.

"We'll chat with people, but mostly, let's listen in on conversations." Jenna headed for the open doors. "To start with, I'll wander around outside on the terraces."

"We should watch for people who seem to be in serious conversations, maybe whispering with others." Ellie checked her watch. "Let's rendezvous back here in an hour and assess our findings."

"I think I'll take the dining room." Courtney smiled. "I'm starving."

"Who's surprised by that?" Angie looked at Mr. Finch. "Where would you like to start?"

"I was thinking of returning to the room where the service was held. Since most everyone is out here, that room would be empty and a perfect spot to run into some people having private conversations." Finch tipped an imaginary hat to Angie and headed in the direction of the memorial room.

Standing alone at the side of the living space, Angie took a deep breath and scanned the crowd. She didn't understand why she felt so nervous. It couldn't just be because Kimberley seemed threatening the other night and she might run into her today. Angie had been in worse confrontations and they hadn't left her feeling so uneasy. She wished Josh had been invited. She hadn't seen him for a few days and missed being with him.

The way Bethany had described the attendees as "snakes" did not encourage mingling with them. Angie just wanted to flee out the front door and sit in a quiet garden, but she knew she had to help find the killer, so reluctantly, she squared her shoulders and moved slowly towards a few people standing near the doors. As a waiter walked by, she removed a glass of champagne from his tray and took a tiny sip in order to appear to be just another mourner invited to the gathering.

She nonchalantly stepped around the periphery of the crowd trying to pick up on what people were saying, when she bumped shoulders with someone. Turning to apologize, she came face to face with Kimberley Hutchins. The two made eye contact. Angie kept her face neutral and didn't say anything. After a moment, she turned away and took a step in the opposite direction.

"Listen." Kimberley spoke. "Forget about the other night, would you? I was in a mood. I was rude."

Angie looked back at the young woman. She felt emboldened by Kim's attempt at an apology so she decided to ask some questions. "What had you so angry?"

"Just this whole mess. Nelson. Having to start a new job. Everything." Kimberley flapped her hand in the air. "I've been stressed."

"Did you work closely with Nelson?" Angie studied Kim's reaction.

"Yes. I did." Kimberley turned to face the windows.

Angie pressed her luck. "Do you think the murderer is here at the reception?"

Kimberley's head jerked around. "How would I know?"

"You worked at the firm. Maybe you heard things. You were privy to information."

"So?" Kimberley's cheeks looked flushed. "The killer didn't waltz over to me and introduce himself."

Angie narrowed her eyes. "Him?"

Kimberley's forehead creased with a quizzical expression.

"You said, 'him.' Couldn't the killer be a woman?" Angie knew she was walking a thin line. She expected the young woman to whirl and storm away at any second.

Kimberley pushed her hair back over her shoulder. "I suppose so. I suppose it could have been a woman. Who knows?"

"I've heard that Nelson had numerous affairs."

Kim's cheeks reddened. "I ...I didn't pay attention to that sort of thing."

"I wonder if one of Nelson's affairs became angry enough with him to...." Angie let her words trail off.

"I ...well, I suppose that's possible." The young blonde stammered.

Angie took a step closer. "How do you know Todd Moore?"

"Through Bethany. She and Todd are friends." Kim spoke hurriedly. "Sometimes a big group of us would go out after work."

"Did you and Todd ever date?"

"What? No. He's just an acquaintance."

Angie was trying to fluster Kim in an attempt to get her to slip and say something incriminating. "You seemed to be having an angry discussion when I saw you with Todd on the restaurant terrace the other evening. Was everything okay? Was he pressing you for information or something?"

Kimberley's eyes flashed and Angie wasn't sure if it was directed at her or was because Kim was angry about her conversation with Todd.

"It was nothing. We were both upset over Nelson." Kim started to unzip her handbag, stopped, and closed it again with a shaky hand, a look of alarm on her face.

A flash of anxiety skittered over Angie's skin, but she took a step forward. "Did you ever date Nelson?"

Kim shuffled two steps back. The red of her cheeks had spread down her neck. Her eyes flicked about the room as she shook her head. "No," she said firmly. "I did not." The heels of her shoes clicked on the wood floor as she hurried away.

A voice spoke behind Angie. "Looks like your attempt at making a friend has failed." Jenna came up and stood next to her sister. Angie told her about the exchange with Kimberley.

"Interesting. I came up empty in my meanderings around here. I didn't hear anything of use." Jenna stifled a yawn. "Who knew rich people were so boring." She smiled. "I'm going to the dining room to grab a bite to eat. You want to come?"

"I'm not hungry. I guess I'll wander around in here for a while longer. Come back after you've eaten and let's join forces."

Jenna headed away for some food. Angie stayed near the windows as she continued her walk around the room. After a few minutes, she stopped and glanced at the groups of people standing around chatting.

A woman spoke to Angie. "I hate these things."

Angie turned. She gave the woman a shrug. "I can't find anyone I know."

"I saw you talking to Kim Hutchins. You know

her?"

"Not really. I've only just met her. We're staying at the same bed and breakfast. How do you know her?"

"I work at Rider Financial. Kim used to work there until recently."

Angie said, "Kim told me she'd given her notice."

The woman gave Angie a surprised look. "Really? That's what she told you? Nelson let her go."

"He did? Why?"

"He had a thing for her, but she didn't reciprocate the feelings. Nelson thought it best to end their association. It wasn't done out of anger. Nelson seemed to really care for her. Kim was leaving the company at the end of the month. Don't spread that around. Obviously, it isn't common knowledge."

"Did you work with Kim?"

"Not really." The woman took a swig of her wine. "We'd cross paths. She was always busy with Nelson."

"What do you mean? You said Kim didn't reciprocate Nelson's feelings."

"Kim traveled with Nelson. She was his assistant. She kept his appointments, shuffled him to meetings, researched and wrote his reports, made sure he knew what to say to clients."

Angie raised an eyebrow. "You make Nelson sound incompetent."

"Not so much incompetent, but lazy and disinterested in his work." The woman finished off her wine and removed another glass from the waiter's tray as he walked past. "Nelson didn't achieve his potential. He was a party-boy. Always chasing women. If he spent more time sober, he might have been successful."

"He was successful at the firm, wasn't he?" Angie played dumb.

The woman gave a knowing grin. "If it wasn't a family firm, he would have been fired. If he didn't have Kim keeping him on track and doing his work for him, even his family wouldn't have put up with him much longer. Poor Nelson." The woman drained her glass. "I'm going to look for another drink." She raised her empty drink glass to Angie and walked away.

Jenna returned just then and Angie told her what the woman said about Nelson.

"She sounds like she had a few drinks too many." Jenna watched the woman in the distance. "Maybe her perception of Nelson isn't accurate. Then again, maybe it is."

"Want to go outside for a breath of fresh air?" Angie led her sister through the open doors.

The sisters wandered onto one of the terraces and they spotted Ellie and Courtney sitting on a bench on the lawn under an apple tree. The girls followed the granite steps down into the garden and they squished together with their two sisters on the bench. Other attendees stood in small groups on the lawn mingling with other guests.

"We needed a break," Ellie said. "It's lovely out here."

"We needed a break, too." Angie admired all the flowers blooming in the manicured beds.

Jenna squinted. "Look over there. It's Bethany and Todd. Over by the pond."

Angie sat up and peered across the lawn at the two people chatting amiably standing by the garden's water feature. "I wouldn't have known that woman was Bethany."

Jenna watched them. "She looks so...."

"Happy," Courtney noted.

"Relaxed." Jenna could see the difference in Bethany's posture and the way she held herself. Next to Todd, she seemed at ease, lighter, comfortable.

"See how they look at each other. It's so sweet." Ellie fiddled with the ends of her blonde hair, and the corners of her mouth turned up in a little smile. "She seems very different around Todd than she normally behaves."

One of the wait staff approached and said something to Bethany, and she turned and followed the woman back into the house. As soon as Bethany moved away from Todd, her posture became stiff and authoritative and her movements were crisp and business-like. Even her face looked different, with the muscles of the jaw appearing hard, giving off a stern, harsh expression.

"Now she looks like the Bethany we know." Angie watched the young woman climb the stairs to the terrace and disappear into the house. The transformation in Bethany as she walked away from Todd made Angie's heart ache. "So which is the real Bethany?"

"Probably both." Ellie watched the platinum blonde hurry through the doors into the mansion. "But the business-like one is the person who is expected to show up most often."

"Come on, enough goofing off." Jenna stood up. "Let's get back to work."

"Into the viper pit we go." Courtney put her arm over Jenna's shoulders.

As Angie and her sisters climbed the stairs back to the house, a thought flickered in her mind and she turned to Ellie. "If someone can change from happy and loving one moment, to hard and brittle the next minute, could that person change into a killer in order to get what they want?"

A worried look passed over Ellie's face. "It does seem possible, doesn't it?"

Anxiety pricked at Angie's skin. "We'd better keep a close eye on Ms. Bethany Winston."

When they entered the house, Jenna and Ellie headed one way and Angie and Courtney went in the opposite direction. They spotted an older man talking to Nelson's sister, Georgia Rider. He gave her a hug and then moved away.

"Let's go offer condolences to Nelson's sister." Angie led the way, and when they were next to Georgia, they introduced themselves.

"How did you know Nelson?" Georgia had a glass of wine in her hand. Her eyelids looked heavy.

The girls hesitated and were about to say that they were friends of Bethany, when Georgia's eyebrows went up. "Oh, are you the young women Chief Martin spoke to me about? The Roselands, right?"

Courtney and Angie both blinked, surprised that the chief might have mentioned them.

"He said he had some consultants who would be speaking with me. Young women."

"Yes." Courtney gave a friendly smile. "Chief Martin calls us in at times to help out."

Georgia's eyes widened and she took a step closer. She lowered her voice. "Are you psychics?"

Angie's face paled and she nearly shouted. "No."

Courtney kept her composure. "Why do you ask that?" She knew Chief Martin would never have revealed their skills to anyone who was not in law enforcement.

"I've heard that sometimes police will call in someone who has special abilities to assist in solving a crime." Georgia looked hopeful. "I wondered if this might be the case with you."

"No, we're not psychics," Courtney said. "I'm surprised. I wouldn't think someone like you would believe such things."

Georgia gave Courtney a cold look. "Someone like me?"

Angie cleared her throat. "My sister only means that most people don't believe in anything like special powers."

"I was hopeful that a miracle would occur and Nelson's killer would be caught." Georgia dabbed at her eyes. "Do you believe in special powers?"

Angie gave an uncomfortable shrug of one shoulder and fibbed. "I've never given it much thought."

Georgia glanced around and then whispered. "Sometimes I sense things. Out of the blue. I wish I was better at it."

Angie's back felt like a cold hand was sliding down along her spine. The tiny hairs on her arms stood up. She chose her words carefully. "Do you? How interesting. Do you sense anything about your brother's death?"

Georgia looked off out of one of the glass doors. "Sometimes I get a sensation." She turned back to Courtney and Angie. "But then it's gone." She shook her head sadly.

Angie asked, "Were you and Nelson close?"

Georgia smiled. "I loved Nelson. He was much younger than I am. I doted on him when he was little. I tried to guide him as he was growing up, help him make the right choices." Her eyes clouded. "I guess I didn't do a very good job."

Angie wasn't sure how to respond to that statement, so she decided to ask some questions. "I understand Nelson was about to announce a run for the Senate."

Georgia smiled sweetly. "He was."

"Was he excited by the prospect of a run for office?"

Georgia's brown eyes pierced Angie's. "Of course."

"I was just wondering what prompted his decision." Angie held the woman's eyes. "A run for office can be difficult. Your life becomes an open book."

"Nelson had nothing to hide. He was a happy, accomplished, well-adjusted man." A serene smile played over Georgia's lips.

Distrust skittered over Angie's skin from what seemed like lies slipping like snakes from this powerful woman's mouth. Angie's impression was that this sister either didn't know her younger brother very well or she was a very good liar.

Courtney looked at Georgia. "Were you in Sweet Cove the night Nelson died?"

"No, I wasn't. I was in New York. My brother, Geoffrey, called me with the terrible news. I couldn't believe it."

Courtney continued. "Do you have any idea who could be behind this? Did Nelson have enemies?"

"Nelson was a sweetheart. Everyone loved him."

Obviously not everyone, Angie thought. "We've

heard he enjoyed partying."

"Nelson was young. Doesn't every young person party sometimes?"

Angie felt chilled and anxious, shaken by Georgia's comment about psychics and her seemingly false statements about her brother. Georgia moved one hand to her shoulder and rubbed at the tension gathered there. The movement caused her expensive, Chanel shoulder bag to slip to the floor with a thunk. Some of the contents spilled onto the floor. Georgia and Angie bent to gather up the items.

"I've been so clumsy lately."

Angie picked up a small wallet, lipstick, a cancelled train ticket, and a pack of tissues and handed them to Georgia. Just then an older couple approached to speak with the blonde woman and Angie and Courtney moved away into the crowd.

Courtney whispered. "She's weird. She either didn't know her brother at all, which I doubt, or she's very good at spinning a fictional story about how great Nelson was."

"I wonder if she's had too much to drink." Angie tried to shake off her unease. "She freaked me out with that question about us being psychics."

The two girls decided to separate in order to cover more territory. As Angie walked around the crowd in the living room trying to eavesdrop on discussions, the core of her body went cold again as if a flood of ice water had shot through her veins.

The suddenness of the sensation made her woozy and she reached out to grasp a side table. Taking some deep breaths, she realized she hadn't seen Mr. Finch in some time and a flash of worry washed over her. She turned towards the far end of the living area to the room where the memorial service was held. Her heart thundered.

Something was wrong. She walked briskly towards the entrance of the room and with each step her feelings of dread ratcheted up a notch. When she was halfway across the living room, a black cat ran from the room on the far side of the space, stopped in her tracks, and swiveled her head searching the living area.

Circe!

Angie and the black cat made eye contact. The creature whirled and raced back from where she had come. Angie's heart jumped into her throat. She bolted across the room in record time.

CHAPTER 14

Angie burst into the enormous room where the memorial service had been held. A man stood a few feet from her. "The service is over. We're cleaning up in here."

"Did you see an older man come in? He walks with a cane." Angie panted from the adrenaline rushing through her body.

The worker looked blankly at the young woman.

"Did you notice a cat? Black. She just came in here."

He glanced about the space. "No cats in here."

Angie ignored the man and rushed further into the room. "Circe! Mr. Finch!" She peered under the seats, looked behind the podium, spun about trying to find Finch or the cat. Thrumming started to beat in her veins. She stopped short, and then turned slowly in a circle. She saw a partially closed door on the other side of the room. She hurried over, and grabbed the knob.

"No one's supposed to be in here now." The man called to Angie. "Miss, you need to go back to the main reception room."

Angie shouted, "Call the police." She pushed open the door and stepped into a dark hallway. Sweat trickled down her back. She edged along the space. "Mr. Finch! Circe!" She caught herself in mid-yell realizing she was foolishly announcing her presence.

After advancing down the hall several yards, Angie heard the meow of a cat. She ran forward and again heard Circe's mew. It came from a room on the right side of the hallway.

She peeked into the large space that was decorated as a den and she saw Circe leaning over Mr. Finch prone on the Oriental rug in front of a massive desk. Angie's blood roared in her ears. She rushed forward and knelt. She felt for a pulse. The side of Mr. Finch's head was covered in blood.

Angie whispered. "Mr. Finch." She could feel the faint beat of a pulse on his neck. "Who did this?" she mumbled.

Circe licked the man's cheek.

"Good Girl." Angie's voice trembled. "Sweet cat."

She pulled out her phone and placed an emergency call for an ambulance and then she texted Jenna. While she sat on the floor next to Mr. Finch holding his hand and whispering his name, tears formed in Angie's eyes and fell, one by one, onto the older man's wrinkled face.

After several minutes passed, which seemed like

hours to Angie, she heard Jenna's voice shouting for her. She directed her sister to the den by calling out.

Jenna rushed in, her eyes wide, her face pale. She knelt beside Angie. "Is he...?"

"He's alive. I can feel his pulse."

Mr. Finch stirred. He turned his head to the side and coughed. His eyes popped open and he winced. "What...?"

"It's okay." Angie squeezed his hand. "Medical help is on the way. You hit your head. You're going to be fine." She didn't think Finch hit his head at all, but she wanted him to remain calm.

Finch blinked his eyes and shifted his gaze about the room. He looked at the girls and kept his voice low. "Someone hit me. Hard. On the head. I went down. And now, here I am."

Angie's lips turned up in a little grin. "So you are. You had me worried."

Finch's voice was hoarse. "You won't get rid of me that easily, Miss Angie."

Jenna tried to lighten the mood. "Did you get a punch in before you went down, Mr. Finch?"

"I don't recall, but I certainly hope so." He managed a smile.

Circe licked the man's face again and lay across Finch's chest.

"My protector." Finch's eyes were soft looking at the black cat. He stroked the soft fur of her back.

"Did you get a look at who hit you?" Angie's

forehead was creased.

"I'm afraid I did not." Finch put a hand to his forehead. "I feel a bit woozy."

Courtney and Ellie rushed in and joined the others on the floor.

Courtney ran her hand gently over Finch's cheek. "You're not supposed to take on the bad guys single-handedly, you know."

Finch smiled at the young, honey-blonde next to him. "Sometimes I can't help myself."

Ellie tried to say something, but her voice cracked and she remained quiet. Tears ran down her cheeks.

Finch saw Ellie's distress. "Now, now, Miss Ellie. I'm a tough old bird."

"I'm supposed to be comforting you." Ellie blubbered.

A police officer rushed in, followed by the emergency medical techs who shooed the girls and the cat to the side while they checked Mr. Finch. Bethany, Senator Winston, and three people Angie didn't know hurried into the room.

Bethany gasped when she spotted Finch's bloody head.

The techs sat Finch up and tended to the whack at the side of his head, determining that some stitches would be needed. They loaded him onto a stretcher.

"I'm going with him." Ellie moved forward. She pulled the car keys out of her small handbag and handed them to Jenna.

"Can I come, too, Mr. Finch?" Courtney winked at him. "I've never ridden in an ambulance."

"I'd be pleased to have your company, Miss Courtney."

Courtney bent and picked up Mr. Finch's cane, and for a second, as she held it, a little buzz of electricity pulsed in her hand, and then the sensation was gone. Angie felt something in the air and made eye contact with her youngest sister. Courtney looked down at the walking stick, turned back to Angie, and shrugged.

As the entourage left the room, Jenna called to the techs. "Take good care of him."

The officer took statements and then told Jenna and Angie, "Chief Martin is meeting Mr. Finch at the hospital to question him about what happened."

Angie nodded and the officer stepped to the other side of the room to speak with Senator Winston. She noticed Detective Lang, the police official she'd met at the crime scene. She raised an eyebrow. He nodded to her and walked over.

"I didn't think detectives answered emergency calls."

Lang spoke softly. "There was an earlier call from this residence. An anonymous caller. Someone reporting that they'd seen a gun in Kimberley Hutchins' handbag."

Angie remembered feeling odd when she was talking with Kim. "And? Did you find anything?"

"I spoke with her shortly before we came in here." Lang made a small gesture toward the floor where Finch had fallen. "Ms. Hutchins' purse was empty. She was upset about being searched." He glanced over at the police officer and excused himself.

Bethany moved to stand next to Angie and Jenna. "Finch must have seen something. Or heard something. It must be Nelson's killer who did this." Her fingers shook as she placed her hand against the side of her face.

Angie took a look around the room. There were two leather chairs placed in front of three wide windows that overlooked the lawn and flower gardens. There was the huge desk in the middle of the room and a large leather sofa against the back wall. Behind the desk were built-in bookcases filled with leather-bound volumes. She shifted her gaze to the back right corner of the room where a white staircase with gleaming wooden treads stood.

Angie startled. Euclid sat at the bottom of the steps. He arched his back, hissed, and raced up the stairs.

Angie and Jenna rushed to the staircase with Bethany at their heels. The police officer and Detective Lang noticed the girls hurry and followed after.

Senator Winston blustered. "What's going on?"

The stairs led to a second floor room with white walls, white sofas, and a wall of huge plate glass windows with views of the back of the property. Euclid sat in front of a closed closet door.

"What is it, Euclid?" Angie's head buzzed. Her palms were clammy and she felt drops of sweat trickling down the side of her face. She took shaky steps towards the cat. Jenna was inches from her sister's back.

Bethany followed. "What's going on? What's with the cat?"

The police officer put his hand on the handle of the gun in his holster. "Hold on. Step back. I'll open it." He moved forward and reached for the doorknob.

Euclid stepped away.

The officer pulled the door open.

The closet was empty.

Except for the gun lying on the middle of the floor.

CHAPTER 15

Jenna and Angie drove to the hospital and picked up Mr. Finch and their sisters from the emergency room. Finch was given twenty stitches and some pain medication. On the way home, he sat on the van's second row of seats with two, furry guards sitting next to him. One was a sleek, black cat and the other was a huge orange boy whose tail lay across Finch's lap.

The girls insisted that the older man stay overnight with them at the Victorian and, since there was time before everyone headed off to bed, they escorted Finch into the living room where they brought him tea and cookies, a fluffy, soft pillow, and a cozy blanket to drape over his legs. The cats perched on either side of him.

"Strange," Finch said. "But I have a craving for boiled eggs."

Shortly after his statement, Ellie carried in a tray with several hard-boiled eggs, a salt shaker, and buttered toast.

The girls sat down around Mr. Finch except for

Courtney who sprawled on the floor in front of the sofa with a bowl of cereal. They discussed the strange events of the late afternoon and evening.

"What were you doing just before you went down?" Jenna asked. "Do you recall what happened right before you got bonked on the head?"

Finch looked off across the room trying to remember. "Things are fuzzy."

"The doc said you might remember more as days pass." Courtney spooned cereal into her mouth. "Your brain got jarred. It needs some time to rest and heal."

"I do recall wandering around the main living room listening to conversations. Something caught my ear." Finch thought for a moment. "But its significance eludes me."

"You'll remember eventually." Ellie poured more tea into his cup.

"I went into the room where the memorial was held. There were people here and there around the room, chatting in small groups. I recall going into the hallway that led to the den. If someone questioned why I was there, I planned to say I was in need of a bathroom. But I can't remember what drew me into the hall."

"Were the cats with you then?" Angie asked.

"No, they weren't. They must have sensed my distress and found me after the attack."

Euclid trilled at the man.

Mr. Finch rubbed his temple as he gave the orange cat a slight smile.

Jenna noted the fatigue on Mr. Finch's face. "I think we've had enough excitement for the day. Why don't we talk about something else? Something more pleasant."

Angie's phone buzzed and she reached to the coffee table to pick it up. She read the text.

"What is it?" Ellie saw the look on her sister's face.

"It's Chief Martin. Preliminary inspection indicates that the gun found in the closet at the Winston's rental house is consistent with the weapon involved in Nelson Rider's murder."

"So." Courtney put her empty bowl on the table. "Who hid it there? Was it Kim?"

"And who called in the anonymous tip to the police about her having a gun in her purse?" Ellie held her hands in her lap. "Was it a hoax or was it legit?"

"And *why* hide the gun there?" Jenna tapped her index finger against her chin.

"All of the people on our list of suspects were attendees at the memorial." Angie pondered. "Any one of them could have tried to dispose of the murder weapon by hiding it in the rental mansion."

"It makes sense to hide it there." Ellie's fingers worried at the ends of her long hair. "If it was well-hidden, which it wasn't, it may have been some time before someone discovered it."

"My bet is that Mr. Finch interrupted the hiding of the gun, so the person had to be quick and haphazardly placed it in the closet." Courtney stretched out on the floor. "Maybe the person intended to return later and hide it properly."

"That's good thinking." Jenna nodded. "Let's talk about the suspects. Let's go over what we know."

"For me, a strong suspect is Bethany Winston." Ellie listed her reasons. "She is smart, resourceful, and determined. She loves Todd Moore and did not want to marry Nelson. She was backed into a corner. Her father seems to have directed her entire life. She probably felt desperate. Eliminate Nelson and be free. Plus, Bethany's a lawyer. She knows how trials and evidence work. She could easily have planned the murder since she must have known when Nelson was in his bungalow."

"What about Todd Moore?" Courtney scratched Circe's cheeks. The black cat had jumped off the sofa and curled next to Courtney on the floor. "He sure had reason to want Nelson dead. Nelson was going to marry the woman he loves."

Jenna said, "What about the threatening letter that Todd got? Who sent it? The sender could be responsible for Nelson's murder. Maybe Todd is next on the person's hit list."

"I didn't think of that." Angie's eyes were wide. "Todd could be in danger."

"Don't forget that we saw Todd and Kimberley in

a heated discussion on the terrace of the restaurant down near the beach." Jenna reminded the group. "What was that about? Are those two working together?" No one had an answer to that. "Who do you think is the most likely suspect?" Jenna poured herself some tea from the pot on the table. "Ellie thinks its Bethany. Does anyone else feel strongly one way or the other?"

Angie sighed. "I'm just not sure. Bethany worries me. She seems to have an answer for everything. But then, there's Kimberley, the spurned other woman. Maybe she was infuriated by Nelson's treatment and she decided to finish him off. And, what about Nelson's family? Nelson made costly mistakes at the family firm and it doesn't sound like it was an isolated error. Could his brother or sister have tired of his foolishness and got rid of him once and for all?"

Mr. Finch held his cup and saucer on his knee. "As yet, no one person stands out. Do we know where these suspects were the night of the murder? Where were they at the time Nelson was killed?"

The girls looked at Finch with blank expressions.

"Perhaps Chief Martin should be consulted," Mr. Finch suggested. "Are alibis solid? Is there someone who doesn't have an alibi? Who has knowledge of guns and how they operate? Mr. Rider was killed with a shot to the head. I assume that the man was asleep at the time since the killer used a pillow to help silence the shot. It wouldn't require much skill to shoot a sleeping man, but it would require some familiarity with a gun."

"I'll talk to the chief tomorrow." Angie felt remiss for not coming up with those questions herself. She looked at Mr. Finch. "Do you have suspicions about anyone in particular?"

"Yes, I do."

The four girls leaned forward waiting for Finch to reveal his suspect.

"The person who knocked me over the head."

The front door of the Victorian opened and Kimberley Hutchins walked into the foyer, the key to her B and B room in her hand. She spied the gathering in the living room and nodded to them.

Euclid arched his back and hissed. Kim looked at the cat with a worried expression. Her eyelids looked heavy with fatigue. She headed for the staircase to go to her room, but she stopped before heading up and looked over at Mr. Finch. "I heard you got hurt at the service. Are you doing okay?"

"Yes, thank you." Mr. Finch managed a smile. "I'm nearly as good as new."

"Glad to hear it." Kimberley nodded. She put her hand on the banister and trudged up the stairs.

Circe emitted a low growl.

When they heard the door to Kim's room open and close, Jenna made eye contact with her sisters and Finch. She whispered. "Suspect number one?"

The doorbell rang.

"We have a revolving door here on this house."

Courtney pushed herself up from the floor. "Any guesses who this is?" She walked through the foyer and pulled the door open. Bethany and Senator Winston bustled in past Courtney.

"We're looking for Mr. Victor Finch," the Senator announced without looking at Courtney. His face was slightly flushed. When he spotted Finch sitting on the sofa in the room off of the foyer, he put his hand on the small of Bethany's back and the two hurried into the living room.

Ignored by the Winstons, Courtney rolled her eyes and mouthed. "Hello. Lovely evening. Do come in." She closed the front door and joined the others.

"So sorry for your accident." Senator Winston sat down across from Finch.

"It was an attack, I'm afraid, not an accident." Finch corrected the man.

"Attack? A strong word." The Senator shook his head. "It must have been a misunderstanding of some kind."

"I'm not sure what kind of a misunderstanding would result in Mr. Finch being pummeled in the head and knocked unconscious." Courtney pulled a side chair forward and sat next to the Senator.

Bethany put her hands in her lap. "My father means that whoever caused Mr. Finch's injury must have thought he was an intruder, or some such thing."

"An intruder? If that was the case," Ellie sniffed,

"wouldn't the person have questioned Mr. Finch before deciding to strike him?" She leveled her eyes at the Winstons and her voice carried a tone of authority. "It was an *attack*."

"The police will get to the bottom of it." The Senator dismissed Ellie's comment and looked at Mr. Finch. "In the meantime, is there some way we can be of assistance to you?"

"How do you mean?" Finch's eyebrows knitted together.

"In any way necessary." The Senator leaned slightly forward. "Do you need some recuperation time? We know several very nice spots in lovely areas of the world that would provide you with the needed luxury and attention to help you recover. We'd be more than happy to make some calls and arrange the time away for you. Bring a friend along."

Finch bristled. Perhaps Senator Winston was making the generous offer because he wanted to nip a potential lawsuit in the bud, worried that the older man might decide to sue them since the injury took place at the house they were renting. Whatever the motive, Finch did not like the sensation of being bought-off. "There is nowhere on earth where I would be better cared for than right here." He gestured towards the sisters.

The Senator chuckled, and then caught himself, realizing that Finch was serious. "Well." He cleared his throat. "At the very least, we'd be happy to take care of your medical bills. Don't hesitate to let us know. Whatever you need, we'll manage it for you." Senator Winston removed a card from his wallet and placed it on the coffee table. "Call anytime, anytime at all." He moved to get up.

Courtney gave the Senator a smile. "If you have a few minutes, it would be very helpful if we could chat about a few things."

Senator Winston stayed in his seat. "Chat? About what?"

Courtney said, "About the events of the past days."

Bethany narrowed her eyes. "What is there to talk over?"

Jenna's eyebrows went up. "A murder, for one thing."

Bethany modified her previous statement. "I meant, what hasn't already been said?"

"We have some questions regarding the crime." Courtney straightened in her seat.

"Why would that be something we would discuss with you?" The Senator gave a small shake of his head.

Angie spoke up. "Because, we work with the Sweet Cove police department."

Senator Winston stared at Angie. "In what capacity?"

Courtney responded to the question with what was becoming a routine reply. "We're criminal justice consultants."

135

The Senator was about to question further when Ellie said cryptically, "We have the necessary experience." She folded her hands in her lap. "We're not allowed to say more."

As she turned to the Senator, Angie bit her lip to keep from smiling at Ellie's handling of the situation. "So if you don't mind, we'd like to ask some questions, but if you'd feel more comfortable, before we begin, I can get Chief Martin on the phone and he can reassure you about our authorization."

Senator Winston waved his hand dismissively. "Go ahead with your questions."

Angie explained. "We're just gathering information about the night that Nelson was killed. We're trying to put pieces together. Who was where? What did people see or hear? The smallest thing can often help lead to the killer, so we'd just like to gather your impressions."

The Senator seemed to relax a little.

Angie started by addressing the first question to the Senator. "Could you tell us what you were doing on the night that Nelson Rider was killed?"

"Of course. Nelson and Bethany and I had dinner together at the resort restaurant. We finished up with our meals around nine. After we ate, Bethany went to her suite. She had some work to do on a case she'd been busy with. Nelson and I went into the bar for a drink. Nelson was still jet-lagged, so he decided to retire early and he went back to his bungalow to rest."

"After Nelson left, what did you do?" Jenna asked.

"I had another drink and then headed back to my suite. I had some paperwork to do."

"Once you returned to your room, did you see or speak to anyone else?" Ellie questioned.

Winston's forehead creased. "No one."

"Did you see or speak to Nelson again that night?" Jenna asked.

The Senator shook his head.

"Who informed you about what happened to Nelson?" Angie watched the man's face.

"A police detective knocked on my door. Around eleven, I believe. That's how I got the news."

"You and Nelson were close?" Courtney asked.

A pained look passed over Senator Winston's face. "He was like a son to me."

Courtney shifted her attention to Bethany. "How did you find out about your fiancé's passing?"

Bethany narrowed her eyes. "I went to my bungalow after dinner. I worked for a while, and then I got restless so I went for a drive." She gave Courtney a pointed look. Bethany did not want her father to know about her late evening visit to the Roselands on the night of the murder. "When I returned to the resort, I saw the police there, the crowd gathered. The police notified me."

Jenna posed the next question. "Do either of you know how to shoot a gun?"

Bethany looked like she'd been slapped.

The Senator replied. "We both know how to shoot. We've spent time on the firing range. We've hunted." He cleared his throat. "When a person is in a certain position, well, you understand, it is imperative to know how to defend oneself. I made sure that my daughter was comfortable around guns."

"Can you think of anyone who would want to harm Nelson?" Angie questioned.

"Nelson was a fine young man." The Senator squared his shoulders. "I have no idea who would want to kill him."

Angie looked at Bethany. The young woman shifted her eyes away, gave a shrug of her shoulder, and shook her head.

Senator Winston stood up, and Bethany followed his lead. "That's all we know. I wish we were more help, I really do." He gave Mr. Finch a nod. "Remember my offer for a getaway to ease your recovery. Think it over. Let me know if you change your mind." He took his daughter by the elbow and they walked briskly through the foyer. Courtney followed behind and opened the door for them. She wished the Winstons a good night.

When Courtney returned to her seat in the living room, she blew out a long breath and eyed her family group. "Someone around us knows more than they're telling. I can feel it."

CHAPTER 16

"Good morning." Jenna placed a platter of banana bread on the dining room buffet table.

Kimberley sat at the dining table scowling at her phone while holding her coffee mug. She looked up when Jenna came in and gave her a half smile. She glanced at the floor for her purse and realized she'd left it in her room. "I'm going upstairs to get my bag. I'll be right back. Don't clear my plate." She got up from the table and hurried away to her room.

Jenna moved to where Kim was sitting to replace the creamer with a fresh pot. Reaching to the middle of the dining table, she noticed Kim's phone was next to her plate and she saw that the screen was displaying the woman's bank account information. Jenna's mouth dropped open when she saw the total in Kim's savings account.

The screen darkened as the phone was about to go to sleep. Pretending to be checking the sugar bowl, Jenna took a quick look over her shoulder, and then touched her index finger to the phone

139

screen bringing the data back into view. She eyed the list of most recent transactions and her heart pounded when she noticed a very large deposit credited to Kim's account three days after Nelson Rider was killed. Hearing footsteps on the stairs, Jenna stepped to the other side of the table, removed some used plates, and headed down the hall to the kitchen.

"Guess what." Jenna, breathless, burst into the room so quickly that Ellie jumped.

Courtney had gone to work at the candy store and Mr. Finch was still asleep. Angie was busy mixing cookie dough. She looked up, alarmed by her sister's sudden appearance.

Tom sat at the center island eating breakfast and he swiveled his stool towards Jenna. "What's up?"

Jenna put the dirty dishes she was carrying onto the counter, hurried over to Tom, and slipped her arm around him. She told Tom and her sisters that she'd seen Kimberley's bank account on her phone and reported to them how much was in it.

Angie almost dropped the tray of cookies she was about to put in the oven. "Over a quarter of a million dollars?"

Ellie's blue eyes were like saucers. She stood frozen in the middle of the room. "Is it accurate? Could you have been looking at something other than her bank account information?"

"I'm sure it was her savings account. All but ten thousand dollars of it came in one lump sum, just days ago. How can she explain that?"

Angie thought. "Well, what about an inheritance?"

"It's quite a coincidence that a lot of money went into her account right after Nelson Rider got killed." With his left hand, Tom lifted a forkful of waffle into his mouth. His right hand rubbed Jenna's shoulders and she leaned into him.

"It's very suspicious." Ellie dried her hands on a dish towel.

Angie said, "I'll tell Chief Martin. Maybe he can look into the origin of the money. Find out who it was transferred from."

"I'll bet you that the money will be basically untraceable." Tom took a swallow from his coffee mug. "Big wigs, corporations, drug money can get passed around through so many channels that it becomes impossible to determine the origin. If this young woman received a bundle of cash recently, I doubt anyone will be able to tell you where it came from. Not without a ton of research, and that costs time and money."

"That can't be legal." Ellie scowled.

"Probably not," Tom said. "But it works."

Angie put her tray of cookies into the oven and set the timer. She went to the kitchen island, crossed her arms, and leaned on it. "So, let's assume that Kimberley got paid off for something. It had to be something important since she got a boat-load of money for whatever it was she did. So what are some ideas of what she might have done?"

"Killed Nelson," Jenna said.

Tom offered, "Sold drugs."

"Inheritance?" Angie shrugged.

Ellie rolled her eyes at the suggestion. "That isn't valid," she insisted. "We're coming up with things someone could get paid off for."

Jenna thought of something else. "Kidnapping."

Ellie shook her head. "Let's keep it to things relevant to this particular case."

A few moments passed, and then Angie came up with an idea. "Kim helped someone eliminate Nelson. Maybe *she* didn't kill him, but she assisted in the planning, or the execution of the plan."

"Execution?" Jenna's expression was serious. "Again, Angie comes up with a poor choice of word."

"But the idea has merit." Tom rubbed the back of Jenna's neck to help remove the tension in her muscles.

"Can I be next for a neck rub?" Angie kidded.

"Get your own man." Jenna chided her sister.

"Neck rubs are over. It's time for me to get to work if you're ever going to open that bake shop of yours." Tom smiled at Angie as he reached for his tool belt, and then looked around the kitchen. "Where are the cats?" Euclid and Circe rarely missed the opportunity to supervise Tom's renovation work in the new café.

Ellie piled waffles on a platter to carry to the

dining room. "The cats are in Mr. Finch's room watching over him. I'm sure once he gets up, those two taskmasters will be down to keep an eye on you."

Tom headed off to work. "I'm going to be lonely without them," he half-joked.

***

Ellie promised to watch the jewelry shop while Angie and Jenna met with Chief Martin at the police station. The girls and the chief talked in one of the conference rooms away from listening ears.

The chief drummed his fingers on the tabletop. "This is an interesting development. Someone paid Ms. Kimberley Hutchins handsomely. For something, and probably not something good. As Tom told you, it will likely be difficult to figure out where the money came from. But Ms. Hutchins and I will have a chat." The chief nodded to Jenna. "Good work."

"Any leads on what happened to Mr. Finch at the memorial service?" Angie asked.

"Nothing yet on who might have attacked him, but the preliminary ballistics report suggests the gun found in the closet of the Winston's rental house is the murder weapon."

Jenna said, "Now we need to figure out who put it there."

Angie gave a sigh. "Easier said than done, but I

feel like we're getting closer."

"There's something else I want to share with you." Chief Martin pushed a folder on the table with his finger. "The "tox" report indicates that Nelson Rider had drugs in his system when he was murdered."

"What kind?" A skitter of unease ran over Angie's skin.

"Opioids. Pain killers. It's one more thing that needs looking into."

"How do you mean?" Jenna's head tilted slightly in a questioning position.

"The report shows a high amount of the pain killers present in his body. It opens up another avenue of investigation. Was Nelson using the drugs for legitimate pain relief or was he abusing drugs? If he was using, maybe it was a drug-buy gone wrong that got him killed."

Angie considered this news. "I don't think the Winstons or Nelson's siblings will be very forthcoming about whether or not Nelson was using drugs. It's not something they would want known."

"That would sully the family's reputation." Jenna observed. "It would also cast a shadow on the family firm. Clients might not be thrilled with the idea of trusting their money to someone whose judgment could be clouded by drugs."

"I wanted you to know about this before you go back to the bungalow. It might help when you ... well, when you investigate the premises again."

The chief never knew how to verbalize what the Roseland sisters could do.

"Josh Williams still doesn't know about our skills." Angie didn't want anything about their "abilities" to slip out when they returned to check out the crime scene at the resort. When the time was right, she would have that difficult discussion with Josh and she hoped he would be accepting. Just thinking about bringing the subject up with Josh made Angie break into a sweat. "I'll tell him one day."

The chief's expression was serious. "I'm always careful not to say anything when we're in public. I would never mention your family's skills in front of others."

Angie gave a nod. "We'll share the information about the drugs with Courtney, Ellie, and Mr. Finch. We'll keep it in mind when we go to the bungalow to investigate."

Jenna brought up the subject of alibis. "Is there anyone who doesn't have a valid alibi for the night of the murder?"

The chief rubbed the side of his face. "Senator Winston claims to have been in his bungalow, but he was alone, so who knows if he was there or not. Bethany Winston reported that she was in her suite and then went out for a drive. We know she went to your house to talk to you that night, but we don't know for sure if she was in her bungalow when Mr. Rider was murdered."

They discussed the time line and determined that Bethany was unaccounted for during the time of Nelson's attack. "We considered the possibility that Bethany showing up at our door might have been a way for her to have an alibi."

The chief agreed. "Is there anything else you've discovered that I might not know about?"

The girls thought for a moment and shook their heads.

"I've requested that the interested parties remain in town for a few more days, and if they need to leave Sweet Cove, that they keep me informed of their whereabouts."

Angie said, "We'll keep investigating. We'll see if we can find out anything about Nelson and the drugs and we'll try to find out more about Kimberley and the hefty deposit to her account."

"I'll see you in a couple of days when we meet at the bungalow." They stood up and left the conference room.

On the walk back to the Victorian, Angie experienced such a moment of dread about returning to Nelson's bungalow that she felt light-headed. She didn't understand her deep sense of unease. She tried to shake off the frightening feelings by thinking about Josh and their upcoming bike ride, but she knew the sensation of anxiety would surge up again and she would have to face it.

CHAPTER 17

Angie sat at the dining room table going over her plans to re-open the bake shop. Jenna was working in her jewelry room and Ellie had gone out for lunch with Attorney Jack Ford. Courtney was at the candy shop and Mr. Finch had slept late, ate breakfast at the Victorian while Ellie questioned him about the injury to his head, and read the news on the porch with the cats watching over him. Tiring easily, he was now upstairs resting in his room.

The girls didn't want him alone the first day after getting knocked on the head so he was spending the day at their house. Later he would head to his new home behind the Victorian, to meet his girlfriend, Betty Hayes, to tell her about his adventures of the previous evening.

Angie was making a list of tasks she needed to complete. Fixtures had to be ordered, boxes had to be unpacked, appliances moved in, and food orders needed to be placed.

She was punching numbers into a calculator

when Kimberley Hutchins burst through the front door of the Victorian and rushed toward the stairs. Her eyes looked wild. When she spotted Angie, she hurried to the dining room and stood there beside the table. Beads of sweat covered the young woman's forehead and she was out of breath.

Angie put down her pencil, alarmed by Kim's distress. "What's wrong?"

"I...." A tear escaped from the corner of her eye and she brushed it away. She put her purse on the table and used both hands to push her hair back from her face. Kim took a quick, nervous glance at the front door.

Angie's inner alarm bells were sounding. "The front door locks when it closes. No one can get in without the code or without having the door opened for them." She gestured to the chair next to her. "Why don't you sit? Tell me what's wrong."

Kim slid into the seat. Her face was pale. Angie wondered if, and how much, she was going to share about what was bothering her. The young woman's distress hit Angie like waves on the shore and caused the thrumming to start in her veins. Whenever there was danger, Angie could feel the pulsing beat in her blood that warned her to be on guard.

"I was supposed to meet with the human resource manager of Rider Financial today. He attended the memorial service and he's staying at the Winston's rental house for a few days, so we made an appointment to meet there to have my exit interview. You know, since I gave my notice."

"What's worrying you about the meeting?"

Kim's eyes flicked about the room. "I'm uncomfortable about leaving the firm. I'd prefer to just do the meeting by phone, but the manager said that I need to sign some forms for things like my 401k, and that the exit interview is always done in person."

"Tell him you're leaving town. Have him send you the forms. You don't have to meet with him." Angie knew there was more to Kim's worry than just being nervous about facing former colleagues.

"I *do* have to. They insist."

"Or what?" Angie narrowed her eyes. The young woman didn't say anything. "They can't make you go there. You're done working for them. You quit. They can't fire you or anything. You no longer have to follow the firms' rules and regulations."

Kim's hands shook and tears gathered in her eyes. "I'm afraid of them."

"Why are you afraid?"

"I can't say."

Angie watched the girl's face. "Do you need to talk to the police? I know Chief Martin and...."

Kim cut Angie off. "No." She practically shouted the word. "No police."

Angie let a few moments pass. "Tell me what's going on, then I can help."

"No." The word came out as a whisper. "This is a mess that can't be helped."

Angie had a million questions that she wanted to fire at the woman sitting beside her, but she knew an interrogation would only result in Kim clamming up or bolting from the room. "Is there something you want me to do?"

"Will you come with me to the meeting?" Kim's pale face was covered with blotchy spots and the rims of her eyes were red. "I don't have family. My good friends are in Europe. I'm alone right now. No one will know if I'm in trouble."

Angie's eyes went wide. "What kind of trouble are you expecting?"

"I just don't want to go alone. I want someone with me." Kim's voice cracked.

"Should you bring a lawyer with you?" Angie was about to tell the nervous young woman about her friend, Attorney Ford.

"I just want you to come. Just another set of ears. That's all. That's all I need."

Angie wasn't sure what to say. She thought that attending the meeting with Kim might reveal some important information, but she also had no desire to put herself in danger. For a minute, she wondered if Kim was trying to set her up, pretending to be afraid just to get her into a worrisome situation. Angie cleared her mind trying to pick up on Kim's true intention. All she could feel was the girl's distress. "What time is the manager expecting you?"

"In an hour." Kim wrung her hands.

"Let me check my schedule for the day. Why don't you head up to your room and try to relax and I'll let you know in fifteen minutes if I can join you." Angie forced a comforting smile.

Kim exhaled loudly. She nodded, gathered up her purse with a shaky hand, and went up to her room. Angie darted down the hall and into Jenna's jewelry shop to talk over what just happened.

"I don't know." Jenna's face was lined with worry. "Is it a trap? Is Kim really afraid of the Rider Firm? Is she in danger? Why does she have to go to the mansion?"

Angie shrugged. "I didn't pick up any sensations that she's lying to me or that she's trying to trick me." She gave her sister a grave look. "But I wouldn't stake my life on it."

"I don't think you should go to the Winston house. It's too isolated." Jenna rolled a pencil over her desk top. "Have Kim tell the human resource manager to meet her at the resort. There are plenty of people around there. It would be much safer."

"Good idea, but will the manager go for it?"

"If not, then don't go with her."

"I'll go talk to Kim." Angie went to the foyer and up the stairs to the second floor. She walked down the hall to Kim's door and called her name. No one answered.

"Kim?" Angie called again and knocked on the

doorframe. When there was no answer, she leaned her ear close to the door. She couldn't hear any sounds in the room.

Angie ran down the stairs and stopped short. A chill skittered down her back.

The front door was ajar.

She rushed to the door and pulled it open. Her heart pounding, she stood on the front porch and looked out to the sidewalk. Turning, she noticed Kim's car parked in the Victorian's driveway, but the young woman was nowhere to be seen.

A meow caused Angie to whirl around and look back into the foyer through the open front door.

Euclid sat on the bottom step of the staircase. He turned and galloped up the stairs. Angie followed. The orange cat stopped at Kim's door, waited for Angie to catch up, and when she was beside him, he stood on his back legs and used his front paws to push hard against Kim's unlocked door. It opened.

Angie peeked in, and dread flooded her body. The desk chair was overturned and Kim's purse was on the floor. She looked at the cat and whispered. "What's going on, Euclid? Did someone get in here?"

Two doors down the hall, Mr. Finch, his eyes bleary and his hair sticking up, poked his head out of his room. "Is something wrong, Miss Angie?"

Angie nodded and Mr. Finch, leaning heavily on his cane, came up next to her to see what was so distressing. He looked into the room and saw the chair on its side on the floor.

"Have you seen Kim Hutchins?" Angie asked.

"I haven't."

"Did you hear anything just now? A scuffle? A shout?"

"Nothing, but I was asleep."

The two stepped into the guest room and Angie told Finch about her conversation with Kimberley. They looked about for any indication of why the young woman might have rushed away. They hoped she'd left of her own accord. Mr. Finch held his cane in his left hand and carefully balanced his weight as he bent down to pick up the purse from the floor.

Angie turned. "Maybe we shouldn't touch anything."

Mr. Finch straightened up, a strange, faraway look on his face. The purse was in his hand.

A pulse of anxiety swam through Angie's blood. She took a step towards the man. "What? What is it?"

Mr. Finch dropped the purse. His fingers trembled. He made eye contact with Angie. "I have an inkling of who attacked me last night."

CHAPTER 18

"It was Kim? She attacked you?" Angie whispered.

Finch gave a slight nod. "I'm not positive, but I think it could be her."

Angie plopped down on the bed. "*She* hit you?"

Finch sat down beside Angie. "I felt something when I touched her purse. It was a woman who hit me. Blonde hair."

Angie groaned. "Everyone involved in this case is blonde."

Finch's face was serious. He blinked. "I'm getting some flashes of remembrance." He clutched his cane. "Can we go downstairs and make some tea? Then I can tell you what I remember."

Angie helped him up and they headed for the stairs. "Jenna's downstairs. I'll have her sit with us and you can tell us both what you recall." She settled Finch at the dining table, retrieved Jenna, and then placed a call to Police Chief Martin. After she relayed what had happened, the chief said he would pay a visit to the Winston's rental mansion and have a couple of officers drive around town to see if one of them could spot Kim.

Angie brought tea into the dining room. "Is your memory returning?"

Mr. Finch looked unnerved. He sipped his tea. "I'm having some flashes of insight." The China cup clattered a bit from his shaking hand when he placed it back on the saucer.

"Can you tell us what you remember?" Anger flushed Jenna's cheeks red when she heard that Kim was probably the one who had knocked the older man over the head.

"I was in the main living room of the Winston's rental house walking about and listening to bits and pieces of conversation. A blonde woman brushed past me. I didn't see her face. The crowd blocked my view, but I caught a glimpse of her from the back as she rushed away. She gave off an air of anger and fear. She was in such a hurry." Circe jumped onto Finch's lap and curled there. He stroked the soft black fur. "I decided to follow her. She went into the large room where the service was held. I entered just as she disappeared through the door that led to the hall."

"You followed after her?" Jenna's eyes were wide.

"I did. One of the benefits of getting older is that many people assume that you are feeble-minded and confused." Finch winked. "I have been known to use that to my advantage."

The corners of Angie's mouth turned up.

"So I wandered into the hall planning to act like I was lost and looking for a rest room. No one stopped me. I moved down the hallway listening for any sound that might indicate where the woman might have gone."

"You heard something?" Angie asked.

"I thought I heard a slight sound of movement or a cabinet door closing, so I stepped into the large den off the hall. I turned towards the windows and a bright flash exploded in my brain. That's the last thing I recall. I think it was Miss Hutchins who hit me."

Jenna almost leaped to her feet. "How dare she? That awful, terrible woman. Striking you like that. It's a good thing she's not here. I'd like to get my hands on her."

"Did she have the gun with her? Could you tell?" Angie leaned closer.

"I don't know." Mr. Finch narrowed his eyes, concentrating. "I wonder if I had the opportunity to touch the gun, if I might sense something."

"I'll talk to Chief Martin, tell him what you remember. Maybe he can arrange for you to see the weapon." Angie tightened her grip on her mug. "So Kimberley must be working with someone. Someone wealthy, of course, since she was paid a quarter of a million dollars. Maybe things have gone wrong and that's why she's afraid to meet with anyone from the Rider Firm." Her voice quavered. "Is she the killer?"

"Well, if she didn't pull the trigger, maybe she helped arrange the hit." Jenna's eyes were dark.

Angie's eyes narrowed. "That woman at the memorial service who worked at Rider, she told me that Kim was Nelson's assistant, that she traveled with him, handled his appointments, kept him on track, basically did all of his work. Kim must have known where he was most of the time, so it would be easy to arrange a hit."

"The money she received." Mr. Finch's hands were steadier now. "That is an important link. It will lead to who Miss Hutchins is working with."

Jenna sat up. "We should talk to Todd Moore, if he's still in town. Maybe there are some clues in that heated discussion he was having with Kim on the terrace of the beach restaurant."

"Let's go right now." Angie started to get up, but then she realized that they couldn't leave Mr. Finch alone in the house due to his recent head injury. While she was trying to think what to do, the Victorian's front door opened and Courtney entered the foyer still wearing her apron from the candy shop. Rufus Fudge, her sort of boyfriend, followed in after her. He gave a big smile to the people gathered around the dining table.

Courtney pulled the elastic from her ponytail and her hair fell in loose waves around her shoulders. "What's cookin'?"

"Plenty." Jenna got up. "Angie and I need to go out." She gave her youngest sister a look so she would understand that it was important. "Can you stay here with Mr. Finch until we get back?"

"Of course." Courtney asked Mr. Finch how his head was feeling and she was pleased to hear that he was much better. "Since you're feeling better again, want to watch some crime shows with me?"

Rufus sat down at the dining table with Finch. "Or we could play a game of cards, if you're up to it."

Rufus and Mr. Finch had started playing cards together some evenings after dinner, and they were often joined by Courtney and Tom, who considered themselves cardsharks. Angie, Ellie, and Jenna, and sometimes Jack Ford and Josh Williams would play board games while the card players dueled with one another.

"That would be most pleasant." Mr. Finch's face brightened as Rufus went to the China cabinet to get the deck of cards. Finch gave Courtney a smile. "We could play cards in the family room and watch crime shows with you at the same time."

"Let's do it." Courtney took off her apron and tossed it on one of the chairs. "I'll get some tasty snacks for us. Meet me in the family room."

Angie and Jenna headed for the front door. Jenna called to Mr. Finch, "Try not to beat Rufus too badly."

***

The girls approached the Seagull Inn near the beach and maneuvered around the tourists. Walking into the lobby, Angie asked her sister, "Do you think Todd has checked out?"

"If luck is on our side, then he's still here." Jenna smiled at the clerk behind the reception desk. "Our friend, Todd Moore, is a guest here. We don't think he's checked out yet. Could you ring his room for us?"

"Who should I say is calling for him?"

Jenna hesitated for a second. "Tell him friends of Bethany would like to speak with him."

The man punched some numbers and held the phone to his ear. When the call was picked up, the clerk spoke. "Mr. Moore, there are two friends of Bethany here in the lobby to see you." The clerk listened to the response. "I'll tell them." He placed the phone on his desk. "I'm afraid that Mr. Moore isn't able to come down right now. He said he'd try to catch up with you at another time."

Jenna's smile faded. She thanked the man, and she and Angie walked to the door and left the inn.

"Did you watch as he punched in the numbers?" Jenna squinted from the bright sunlight.

"Yup. 226. Did you see the same?"

Jenna nodded and gestured to the walkway that led to the guest cottages behind the main inn. The girls were familiar with the layout of the inn's rooms and suites from staying sometimes at the hotel when they were children. "Shall we pay Todd a visit?"

When they reached Todd's suite, they knocked, and after a few minutes, Todd opened the door. His face hardened when he saw them. "The desk clerk gave you my room number?" He stepped out and pulled the door closed behind him.

"No, he didn't." Jenna stood straight. "We watched the numbers he pushed when he called you."

"Can we talk with you for a few minutes?" Angie made sure not to use a confrontational tone.

Todd started to make an excuse, but Angie interrupted. She decided not to reveal her suspicions that Kim might be the killer, but instead, use concern that Kim might be in danger to get Todd to talk with them. "Kim Hutchins is afraid of Nelson Rider's family. She had an appointment to meet with them, but she didn't want to keep it. She's staying at our bed and breakfast. I went to her room and the door was ajar. Things were knocked over inside. I worry that she might be in trouble."

Alarm spread over Todd's face. He rubbed hard at his forehead.

"If you don't want us to come in, why don't we go somewhere else," Jenna suggested. "There's a place around the corner. We won't take much of your time."

Todd looked like he was searching for an excuse to avoid the girls. His eyes flicked around the hotel grounds and his breathing quickened. Worried that Todd might take off, Angie took a half step to the right to close the distance between her and Jenna to block Todd's escape route.

Jenna looked at Todd hopefully. "Kim might be in danger. If we could just chat, even for a few minutes, it might help."

Todd let out a quick breath. "There's a place on the corner. A breakfast place, a small café. You know it?"

"Yes. Phil's Restaurant." Angie nodded.

"I need to finish up what I was doing before you knocked. Meet me at Phil's in thirty minutes."

Jenna's eyes narrowed. "How do we know you'll show up?"

Todd opened the door to his suite just a crack. "You don't." He stepped inside and shut the door.

The girls walked slowly down the brick walkway.

"Is he going to show?" Jenna took a look back to Todd's suite.

"Who knows?" Angie checked her phone for messages.

"We need to watch the cottage to see if Todd will try to make a getaway."

"Let's lurk over there behind those trees. We can see if he comes out and if he heads to the café to meet us or if he takes off for the parking lot." Just as Angie was placing her phone back into her purse, it buzzed. She looked at the incoming text. "It's from Bethany. She needs to talk. Right away. It's about Kim Hutchins."

"Tell her to come to Phil's Restaurant." Jenna's mouth turned up in a sly smile. "Then we can talk to Todd *and* Bethany at the same time."

Angie texted a reply asking Kim to come to Phil's, but she did not mention Todd. "Let's see what she says."

A new text came in. "Bethany says she's at the resort and she can't get away. She needs us to come there."

"Should we divide and conquer?" Jenna asked.

"I'll go back to the Victorian and take my bike to the resort. You stake out Todd's suite and see if he heads to the café or not."

Angie hurried away up Beach Street to the Victorian, playing the events of the past days in her mind. Kim Hutchins was looking more and more like she was either the killer or an accomplice. As Nelson's assistant, she knew where and when he would be in a particular place. She must have received the big payout for her role in the murder. Now she was frightened of people associated with the Rider family and firm. Still, something seemed off. The cats didn't like her, but they didn't react like she was a killer. Angie thought that she and her sisters and Mr. Finch needed to go back to the crime scene bungalow and investigate, and the sooner it happened, the better.

She thought about Bethany and Todd, in love with each other, but destined not to be together because Bethany was supposed to marry Nelson. They would both benefit with Nelson out of the picture, which gave them motive to kill.

Was she missing something? Angie blew out a long breath. Something popped into her head and she stopped in mid-step. *Uh oh.*

She whirled and ran down Beach Street back towards the Seagull Inn.

CHAPTER 19

Angie raced into the inn's parking lot and ducked into the corner where a huge Maple tree grew in the lawn at the edge of the hardtop. She was breathing hard. She removed her phone from her pocket and texted Jenna to ask if Todd had emerged from his cottage. When Jenna replied in the negative, Angie asked her to go and knock on his door, and if he didn't answer, see if she could peek in his front window.

After a few minutes, the phone rang.

"No one answers and I can't see in the window. The shade is drawn."

Movement on the other side of the parking lot caught Angie's eye. A woman wearing a big, floppy hat and sunglasses was walking towards some parked cars. Angie turned her attention back to her phone call with Jenna, but before she could say anything, she spun back to take another look at the woman. Something about the posture and the way she moved convinced Angie. She spoke into the phone. "Come to the parking lot. Hurry."

Angie started across the lot. The woman spotted her and broke into a jog, heading for a dark blue Toyota SUV.

"Bethany." Angie called to her. The woman ignored Angie's shout and picked up her pace.

Angie bolted to the SUV and got there just before the woman.

Bethany pulled off her sunglasses, her eyes flashing. "Can't you just leave us alone?"

Angie's anger matched Bethany's. "You want me to forget that a man was murdered? Your fiancé? What are you doing? Running from the crime?" The thought that Bethany could be armed with a weapon jumped in Angie's brain cells, but it didn't deter her. She was outraged that a criminal was about to escape.

Todd jumped from the SUV. "What do you want? Why can't you just leave us alone?"

Jenna ran into the parking lot and headed to where the three people stood near the vehicle.

"Stop, Jenna. Don't come closer." Angie held her palm up towards her sister to warn her to stay back in case Todd or Bethany had a gun. "Call Police Chief Martin."

"No!" Bethany shouted. "We'll talk to you. Don't tell anyone where I am."

Jenna took a look at Angie to see if she should place the call or not.

Angie was torn, but Bethany's desperation caused her to hesitate. She lifted her index finger to have Jenna hold off for a moment.

She looked at Bethany and Todd. "Stand apart from each other. I need to be sure that neither one of you has a weapon."

"What? A weapon?" Bethany scowled and placed her hands on her hips. Her eyes were like saucers. "You think *we* killed Nelson?" She threw her head back and put her hand to her forehead. "We did not. I swear to you."

"Why are you running away then?" Angie demanded.

Todd stepped close to Bethany and took her hand. "Beth and I are done with the way things have been. We're leaving to make a life together. Nelson's murder ... I know it's a stupid cliché, but life is short."

Bethany rested her head on Todd's shoulder. "We want to spend our lives with each other." She gazed into Todd's eyes. "We're going to be together. I don't care if my father disowns me. I'm not playing by his rules anymore."

"You can't just take off," Angie warned. "Hasn't Police Chief Martin asked you to stay in town for a few more days? Aren't you supposed to tell him if you leave the area?"

Jenna had come up to stand next to her sister. "If you two run away, it will make you look guilty. You'll be prime suspects. The police will be sure you killed Nelson."

All the joy was sucked from Bethany's face.

"But...." She couldn't finish her sentence because she knew that Jenna was right. "We can't stay here. I can't be around my father right now. I can't tell him in person that I'm marrying Todd. He will need time to cool off before I can face him."

Angie had an idea. "There's a carriage house behind our Victorian. There's an apartment you can use. Stay there for a day or two. Take the time to think things through and if you decide to leave, then tell Chief Martin. We can take you to the apartment right now." She narrowed her eyes. "But you need to talk to us once we get there."

Bethany and Todd exchanged glances and nodded.

They all piled into Todd's vehicle and made the short drive to the Victorian.

CHAPTER 20

Angie and Jenna informed their two sisters what had gone on in the parking lot of the inn near the beach and that Bethany and Todd were now guests in one of the carriage house apartments.

"I'm inclined to believe them when they say they had nothing to do with Nelson's murder." Angie hoped she didn't regret that statement.

"Bethany's taking a big risk to run away with Todd. Her father will probably go ballistic." Ellie set the table with cups and saucers and dessert plates.

"Wow, two people in love, running away from adversity." Courtney's eyes looked dreamy. "It's very romantic."

"Running from trouble usually doesn't solve things, it just postpones it, or makes it worse." Jenna sat at the table with her chin in her hand. "Speaking of romance, where's Rufus?"

"He's having dinner with Jack Ford." Courtney smiled. "Then he's coming back here and we're going out. Mr. Finch went home to meet Betty.

Rufus and I walked him home to be sure he got there safely."

A knock sounded at the front door. Courtney walked through the foyer and opened the door to Bethany and Todd who entered hand in hand. Everyone sat down around the dining table where tea, coffee, and wine were available, along with several plates of appetizers and dessert squares.

"I hear you're going to be married." Courtney smiled at the couple.

Bethany beamed at Todd. "This time it's a *real* marriage. This time it's for love."

Angie hated to spoil the mood, but she had to ask some questions. "What do you know about Nelson's death?"

Bethany's facial muscles drooped. "Just what you know. I didn't find out he was dead until we all left your house and returned to the resort that night."

Todd squeezed her hand. "It was a shock. I hate to say it, but one night, in desperation, we talked about how things would be if Nelson was dead."

Bethany looked at Angie and Jenna. "When you told Todd that Nelson had been killed, for a little while, he feared I might have done something terrible so that we could be together." She touched her hand to Todd's cheek. "And when I first heard about Nelson's murder, I had the same fear that Todd might have taken matters into his own hands and done something horrible."

Courtney addressed Todd. "We saw you and Kimberley Hutchins in a heated discussion on the restaurant terrace down near the beach. Can you tell us what you were talking about? How did you end up meeting?"

Todd turned his eyes to Bethany. "I contacted Kim and asked her to meet me to find out what she knew about Nelson's death. I demanded to know if she knew who killed him." He turned back to the girls. "I was terrified that Beth had done it so that we could be together."

"What was Kim's response?" Angie asked. "Did she reveal anything to you? Does she know anything?"

"She denied knowing anything about what happened. I pressed her. I know she was Nelson's assistant. I thought she might have some inside information, but she claimed ignorance, so we went back and forth at each other. She seemed nervous. I was sure she was hiding something. She just kept saying she didn't know anything, so I stormed out."

Angie turned to Bethany. "Kim traveled with Nelson, right? Someone I spoke with implied that Kim was sort of Nelson's handler."

Bethany nodded and looked down at the table. "Nelson couldn't stay on task, so the firm assigned Kim to be sure he showed up at meetings when he was supposed to. I think Kim was actually the one who did all of Nelson's work for him. She'd brief him on matters and give him all the details, wrote the reports. Nelson was a quick study. He could absorb material fast, as long as it was handed to him to memorize." She gave a little shrug, and frowned.

Ellie asked, "Why was Nelson so incapable of doing any work? From what people have said, he seemed bright enough. He couldn't have been partying all day and all night."

A shadow of sadness covered Bethany's face.

"Nelson used pain killers?" Angie asked gently. "His issue with pain killers interfered with his work?"

Bethany's shoulders sagged. "He used pain killers heavily. He used other drugs as well. Try as we might, we couldn't get Nelson clean. His brother put Nelson in a facility, a very private facility for the wealthy, to try to help him, but nothing stopped him from using. It took over his life."

"Wouldn't his problems with pain killers have hurt his Senate race?" Courtney asked, thinking about the plans to have Nelson run for office.

Bethany shook her head. "Nelson hid it well. Only the people in his close circle knew and no one would ever find out he was treated at that facility. They are very discreet there because their clientele demands ultimate privacy."

Courtney turned to Todd. "Did Kim say where she was the night Nelson was killed?"

"Kim told me that Nelson's brother, Geoffrey,

gave her the key to Nelson's room so she could check on him if necessary. Geoffrey put Kim up at a hotel near the resort. Kim said she was in her room when Nelson was killed."

A feeling of unease flashed in Angie's chest. She glanced at her sisters to see if any of them were experiencing a similar feeling, but everyone's attention was on Todd. She hated to ask the next questions and braced herself for possible reactions. She cleared her throat and made eye contact with Todd. "Can you tell us where you were at the time Nelson was killed?"

Todd's face went blank. "You don't think I killed him?" He seemed to suck in a breath.

Angie turned her hands palm-side up. "We've only just met all of you. We don't have past history with any of you on which to base our ideas. In order to be thorough, we have to suspect everyone."

"I was in my room at the inn on the beach."

Angie watched Todd carefully. "Do you know what time Nelson was killed?"

The young man opened his mouth and then shut it. He thought for a moment. "Um. It happened in the evening. I guess I don't really know the exact time."

Jenna leaned forward. "When did you arrive in Sweet Cove?"

"The day Nelson was killed. That morning."

"Why did you come to Sweet Cove?" Ellie asked.

"To meet up with Beth. We were going to leave

together. Get away from all this nonsense."

All eyes turned to Bethany.

Angie's brow furrowed. "You had it all planned? To take off before your wedding to Nelson?"

Bethany bit her lower lip. "I know it sounds awful. The whole circus started up and I couldn't think how to stop it. There was no way I was going to marry Nelson, but I couldn't tell my father that. Things were set in motion, like a huge truck barreling down a hillside without brakes. The only thing I could think of was to run away."

"You were going to leave a man at the altar? In front of family and friends?" Courtney couldn't believe her ears.

Bethany shook her head vigorously. "I was going to tell him before the wedding day dawned, to give everyone a couple of days to notify the guests. I would never humiliate Nelson. I *did* care for him." Her eyes looked wet. She blinked hard.

Angie gave Bethany her full attention. "Can you tell us where you were the night Nelson was killed?"

The young woman's eyes widened. "I was here with all of you."

Jenna's voice was soft. "Nelson was killed before you got here."

Bethany shot Jenna a look. "How do you know that for sure?"

Ellie frowned. She didn't care for Bethany's tone. "Because of forensic evidence."

"The police gave you that information?" The

platinum blonde appeared miffed.

"They did." Ellie confirmed. "So please tell us where you were."

"In my room. Until I left to come and see you." The wind seemed to have been knocked out of her sails.

"Can anyone confirm that?" Angie asked.

"I was alone." Bethany's cheeks flushed pink. "So, what? Now you think I'm the killer?"

Jenna sighed. "We need to consider the possibility that anyone might be guilty."

Bethany rolled her eyes and her facial features hardened. "That's not how it's supposed to work." She stood up abruptly and headed for the door. Todd scurried to his feet and followed Bethany out of the Victorian, a look of embarrassment on his face.

The girls sat around the table in uncomfortable silence, each one going over the things that had been said. After a few minutes, the front door opened. The sisters looked up expecting to see Bethany and Todd returning, but it was Kimberley Hutchins who walked into the foyer.

CHAPTER 21

Kim's face was pale. She nodded to the group as she hurried to the stairs.

Angie stood up. "Kim. Are you okay? Where were you?"

Kim held the banister and paused. Her face was pinched with tension. "I'm fine." She turned to climb the stairs.

Angie walked over to her. "Where did you go? I saw the chair in your room overturned. I was worried that something happened."

A sour expression washed over Kim's face. "I have a mother. I don't need another one. You don't need to worry about me." She took two steps up the staircase. "And you shouldn't be in my room."

Angie felt a surge of annoyance and anger. "Hold on. Did you go to the meeting with the Rider human resource manager? You were so worried about seeing him. What happened?"

"I told you, everything is fine." She stormed up the staircase.

Angie called after her. "Hold on. We need to

talk to you."

"I don't have to talk to you." Kim's footsteps pounded across the second floor landing and a loud bang of her door emphasized her refusal to engage in conversation.

Angie's mouth was hanging open. She turned back to her sisters and blinked. "What on earth?" She went back to the dining table and sat down with a sigh. "Am I hallucinating? Was Kim a nervous wreck earlier today? Was she afraid to go to that meeting? Did she rush out of the house so quickly that she knocked over the desk chair? Or did I imagine the whole thing?" She shook her head slowly and waved her hand towards the foyer staircase. "Because Kim sure makes it seem like I made it all up."

Courtney scowled. "Maybe I'll go up there and make her answer our questions."

Ellie said, "You can't do that. She's a paying guest in this B and B. We cannot harass the clientele. Let it go. Her business isn't our concern."

Jenna's brows furrowed. "It might be our concern, if she was involved in killing Nelson Rider and bashing Mr. Finch over the head at the reception."

Ellie twisted the linen napkin in her hands and glanced towards the stairs. "Let the police question her." Ellie gripped her tea cup. "Tell Chief Martin. Let him handle it. I'm afraid of her."

Courtney kept her voice soft. "Chief Martin

doesn't have powers. If we talk to her, we can use our skills to sense if Kim is telling us the truth or not."

Ellie stood and started to gather the used plates. "Well, your skills don't seem to be of much use lately."

Courtney's eyes widened. "Well...." She didn't know how to defend herself because what Ellie said was true. "You should talk," she fired back lamely. The sisters had been experiencing interference in picking up on things. Either they didn't feel anything at all or the clues were being jumbled. Courtney's shoulders drooped.

Angie's phone buzzed and she read the message. She let out a sigh. "I'm going to the resort to meet Josh for dinner. I need a break from all of this."

* * *

Angie sat on a stool at the resort's bar waiting for Josh to finish up with a last minute problem before meeting for dinner. The bartender recognized her and struck up a conversation.

"It's fairly quiet here tonight." Bob wiped the granite counter top with a white cloth. "The past days have been hectic with police and detectives and media milling around."

"It was certainly an unexpected event." Angie shook her head. "People think of the resort as a place for relaxation and fun. A murder is the last thing anyone imagines would happen here."

The bartender poured seltzer into a glass, garnished it with a slice of orange, and placed it in front of Angie.

She took a sip. "Did you happen to meet the victim? Did he ever come in here for a drink?"

Bob leaned an elbow on the counter. "He came in with that Senator, the night he was murdered. They had a drink, and then they parted. Later on, the Rider guy came back. Sat here at the bar, we chatted. He said he was restless and thought another drink might help."

"Did he seem nervous about anything, worried?"

Bob kept his voice low. "He seemed addled, you know, like the way a nicotine addict acts when he needs a smoke. Twitchy, a little tremor in the fingers. The Rider guy had a bit of a glassy-eyed look. You know what I mean? He needed something. Booze, cigarettes, something stronger, maybe."

"Did you have a chance to talk?"

"It was busy that night, but when Rider came in, there was a lull. We shot the breeze for a while, nothing earth-shattering." Bob moved down the bar to wait on a fashionable, young couple who came in and sat down. He made two Martinis for the man and woman and then returned to talk to Angie.

"You know, Angie, the Rider guy said some things I thought were kinda' odd."

Angie cocked her head, questioning.

"Yeah." Bob's forehead creased trying to remember the exact words. "I mentioned something about his upcoming wedding. How did he put it? Rider said something like, 'poor Beth, I don't want to hurt her. She's put up with enough. She doesn't want to marry me either, so no wedding.'"

"Really?" Angie had a tight expression on her face. "He said that?"

"Yup." Bob nodded. He held a beer glass in his hand and dried it with a towel. "Then he said something like, no senate either. Whatever that meant. I figured he was high or drunk and didn't know what he was muttering."

Angie looked across the bar, deep in thought.

"What do you think he was talking about?" Bob asked.

"Did you ask him why he said that?"

"I didn't get the chance. He got a call and left in a hurry. Left me a big tip, though." Bob started away to wait on a group of people who gathered at the far end of the bar.

When he was two steps from Angie, she asked, "Did you tell the police what Nelson said about not wanting to get married?"

Bob looked back and shook his head. "I just, this minute, remembered it."

Angie was so distracted by the thoughts running through her head that she jumped when Josh approached and touched her shoulder. She whirled around and saw him standing next to her, with a warm smile on his face, his eyes kind and caring. All worry dropped away and Angie's muscles relaxed as Josh bent and kissed her lips. They walked arm and arm to the resort dining room and sat at a table near the windows where they talked and mooned over one another. Candlelight flickered over their faces.

By the end of the evening, Angie felt as light as a feather. She hummed as she unlocked the back door of the Victorian and sashayed into the kitchen, with thoughts of Josh dancing in her head.

Courtney stood in the middle of the kitchen holding a spoon in the air in front of Ellie who was seated on a stool at the center island. "Go ahead, try again."

"I just can't do it." Ellie hung her head and her long, blonde hair fell over her face.

Angie's eyes went wide.

Courtney heard Angie come in, but didn't turn to look at her sister. Her arm was outstretched dangling the teaspoon from her fingers. "What's cookin', Sis?"

"I'm about to ask you two that same question. What's going on?"

"Go ahead." Courtney urged Ellie to try again.

Ellie leaned against the counter with her chin in her hand. "We've been practicing for a few days, but I can't do anything."

"Like what? Eat from a spoon that's located twenty feet from you?" Angie smiled and sat down next to her sister.

Courtney lowered her arm. "She just has to believe in herself."

Lifting her head, Ellie groaned. "How did I ever make that bullet soft? How did I bend that gun barrel into a pretzel? Did that even happen?" In a previous investigation, Ellie was instrumental in saving her sisters and Mr. Finch by using her mind to make a bullet as soft as a marshmallow and twist the barrel of a gun like it was rubber. She had never done anything like that before or since.

"I'm surprised that you're talking about what you did, let alone attempting to practice your skills." Angie was amazed that Ellie was practicing because the whole thing had always frightened her.

Ellie's blue eyes were serious. "With all the trouble that's happened over these past months, I thought what I could do might come in handy again someday and that I should be ready. Not that I want to do anything. It scares me. It's just that I worry about all of you."

Angie rubbed her sister's arm. "I think Courtney might be right. Maybe your fear overrides your ability. Like the stupid static is overriding our abilities to understand clues and sense what people have done."

Euclid and Circe trilled from their perch on top of the refrigerator.

Angie looked up at them and she experienced a moment of clarity. "Huh." A slow smile spread over her face. "I wonder. The bad stuff that's been happening, has it weighed us down? Has it made us deaf to the things that float on the air that we can usually pick up on?"

Courtney's eyes widened with excitement. "You haven't baked anything for us for ages. Bake something. Think positive thoughts while you mix. Clear out the heaviness around us from all the bad things we've had to deal with lately. And then, let's take what you bake down to Robin's Point. We'll eat it there where Nana's cottage used to be."

"A picnic in the dark." Ellie smiled as she pulled out a mixing bowl, flour, and measuring cups and piled the things on the island. She halted. "What do you want to make?"

"I haven't agreed to bake yet." Angie laughed as she opened the pantry closet, lifted her apron from a hook, and slipped it over her head.

Mr. Finch came into the kitchen from the back of the house and saw Angie in her apron. "Well, it looks to me like you've made up your mind to bake something. What treat are you making, Miss Angie?"

Angie pulled her hair into a high ponytail and washed her hands in the sink. She turned around and folded her arms over her chest, thinking. Angie had the ability to transfer intentions into what she baked which would then influence the thoughts or feelings of whoever ate the treats. She tapped her fingers on her upper arm. "It needs to be something sweet, but light." She looked at the people in the kitchen. "How about a blueberry-lemon tart?"

"That's perfect." Jenna came in from the hallway with Tom following her. "It's one of my favorites."

"What's the occasion?" Tom carried two empty mugs. He and Jenna had been sipping coffee while rocking on the front porch watching the tourists streaming by on the sidewalk in front of the Victorian.

Courtney explained while Angie went about measuring and mixing. Tom, Jenna, Mr. Finch, Courtney, and Ellie each took a stool at the counter to watch Angie bake. The two cats each kept an eye on the proceedings from high on the fridge.

Angie lifted her eyes from the bowl in front of her to see the audience gathered along the opposite side of the center island and she let out a chuckle. "Maybe I should sell tickets to my performance."

CHAPTER 22

It was midnight when Tom, the four sisters, and the two cats sat down on the blanket that Courtney had spread on the lawn at Robin's Point at the edge of the bluff looking out over the sea. Stars twinkled overhead and a silver path of moonlight streamed over the surface of the ocean and seemed to end at the foot of the cliff.

Tom unfolded a lawn chair for Mr. Finch, and Ellie placed the picnic basket on the edge of the blanket. The girls removed the blueberry-lemon tart, dessert plates, forks, napkins, a silver cake knife and server, and a bottle of champagne that they remembered they had in the refrigerator. They didn't want to bother packing champagne flutes so they took along small plastic cups. Not very elegant, Ellie told the group, but they'd do.

Jenna brought two metal lanterns with a candle in each one. She lit them and placed the lanterns in the middle of the blanket. Angie cut the tart and passed around the plates while Tom popped the champagne and filled the cups.

"We should do this more often." Courtney handed Mr. Finch a cup.

When everyone was served and settled, Ellie suggested a toast. She looked over at Mr. Finch. "Will you do the honors? We need something positive and upbeat."

"That is quite easy to do." Finch cleared his throat. "As I've said many times, I feel like the best part of my life started when I came to Sweet Cove and met all of you."

Courtney interrupted. "Don't forget about Betty Hayes." She winked at Finch.

Finch nodded, and though no one could see, just thinking of Betty caused a blush to tinge the older man's cheeks. He continued with the toast. "And despite our run-ins with the criminal element, I have witnessed honor, friendship, love, and goodness in the people, and felines, around me. I am truly blessed." He raised his plastic glass. "To all of you, my friends."

"Here, here." Tom tapped his cup against Mr. Finch's.

"Well done, Mr. Finch." Ellie's eyes were moist.

Everyone dug into the tart. Even the cats had plates in front of them and they eagerly gobbled the tasty treat.

"I feel better already. Lighter, happier." Courtney sighed and lay back on the grass. "I feel the thrumming. It's good." Five minutes later, she sprang up. "Let's test to see if our love-fest here

185

with the dessert cleared away the static and negative vibrations from our past investigations that were interfering with our powers." Courtney reached for the spoon she had used, licked it clean, and then held it out to her side. She looked across the darkness at Ellie. "Do something to the spoon."

Ellie frowned and her shoulders drooped. "I'm afraid."

Mr. Finch requested that the spoon be passed to him. "There's nothing to fear, Miss Ellie. You use your powers for good." He rested the spoon on his knee. "Close your eyes. Take slow, deep breaths. Imagine the spoon is as light as a feather floating in the ether."

Ellie closed her eyes. Even in the feeble light of the lanterns, the group could see her tense muscles go loose with each deep breath. Sitting cross-legged on the blanket, her upper body started to rock ever so slightly. Angie could feel the thrumming in her veins, pulsing in time to Ellie's swaying motion. She made eye contact with Courtney who gave her sister a slight nod and a smile. Two full minutes passed. Nothing happened.

Angie was about to speak, when the spoon on Mr. Finch's knee began to tremble. Everyone's eyes grew as wide as saucers. Euclid and Circe stared at the utensil.

Slowly, the quivering spoon lifted an inch above Finch's knee and hovered for a moment in the air, until it sputtered and fell to the blanket.

Courtney whooped. Angie's mouth dropped open. The cats trilled and Euclid jumped onto Ellie's lap and licked her cheek as spontaneous applause broke out.

Ellie blinked her eyes. A giggle escaped from her throat. "I did it?"

Everyone hugged her and offered congratulations.

"Just keep practicing." Courtney gave Ellie a bear hug. "Just think how you'll freak out Jack Ford with that trick someday."

Ellie paled at the thought of revealing the Roseland secrets to her boyfriend. She knew that, one of these days, a long conversation was in store. She hoped that Jack would be able to accept the news of her family's skills as well as Tom had when Jenna told him. She pushed the worry from her mind as a second round of champagne was passed around the group in celebration.

✳✳✳

It was after two in the morning when the six humans and two cats stumbled out of Ellie's van in the driveway of the Victorian. Tom kissed Jenna goodnight and got into his truck to drive home. Mr. Finch had been dropped at his house and Courtney walked him to his front door. Ellie, Jenna, and Courtney dragged themselves up to their rooms and two of the sisters would not be pleased when the early morning alarms sounded.

Angie didn't feel tired so she decided to make a cup of tea before following her sisters up to bed. She put the kettle on and started to rinse off the dessert plates from their late-night picnic when she glanced out the window and noticed movement in the moonlight in the backyard near the pergola. She turned the sink faucet off and squinted through the window glass trying to see the person sitting in one of the Adirondack chairs under the trellises. Angie backed over to the stove and turned off the burner, and then she headed out the back door.

She glided with soft footsteps over the walkway that led to the patio under the pergola. "Can't sleep?"

Bethany Winston jerked with surprise. "I didn't hear you. Why are you still up?"

"I had something I had to do." Angie settled in the chair opposite Bethany. "I've been thinking."

Bethany looked over at Angie. "That I'm the killer?"

Angie waited to see if the thrumming would start and contradict her feeling that Bethany was innocent, but there was no warning pulsing. "I don't think you're the one who killed Nelson." Angie could see a look of relief pass over Bethany's face.

"Then who do you think did it?"

"I'm not sure yet." Angie pushed her hair behind

188

her ears. A sudden sense of fatigue washed over her and she let out a small sigh. "I was at the bar at the resort recently. I had a talk with the bartender."

Bethany listened with interest.

"The bartender met Nelson about an hour before he was killed."

Bethany winced at the mention of Nelson's murder.

"Nelson came back to the bar after he and your father had been there a bit earlier. He struck up a conversation with the bartender. The bartender recalled something that Nelson said to him."

Bethany leaned forward. "What was it?"

"Nelson said he didn't want to hurt you. He said he didn't want to marry you any more than you wanted to marry him. He implied that he wasn't going to go through with the marriage."

Bethany's mouth dropped open. "Nelson said that?"

"If you two didn't marry, who would that hurt?"

Bethany tilted her head in thought. "Well, it would hurt his run for the Senate, so it would hurt Kim, for one."

"Why Kim?"

"Kim was going to be his campaign manager, and if he won the race, she was to be his Chief of Staff. She had plenty of experience handling Nelson and that was going to continue in Washington."

"Who else?"

"It would hurt Nelson's brother and sister, Geoffrey and Georgia. They had plans for Nelson in the Senate. Nelson was going to be their puppet." Bethany shook her head in disgust.

"What about Geoffrey? What do you think of him?"

"He makes me uncomfortable. I don't trust him. He wants to be head of the family company and he isn't subtle about it."

"I talked to Georgia at the remembrance. She seemed odd."

"Georgia? Really? She must have been drunk when you talked to her. She loves her wine, but she usually knows when and where it's appropriate to drink. That woman is shrewd, controlling, and highly intelligent. The company's success is because of her, despite what Geoffrey would like people to think. Geoffrey doesn't have a chance against Georgia as top-dog of Rider Financial."

"What about you? If Nelson called off the wedding, would it have hurt you?"

The corners of Bethany's mouth turned up. "No. It would have made me happy. It does make me happy. Nelson was about to call off the wedding." She let out a chuckle. "He was about to stand up for something *he* wanted. Finally."

A thought ran through Angie's mind. *And that's why he's dead.*

CHAPTER 23

An unmarked police van pulled into a parking space under a streetlight in the utility lot of the Sweet Cove resort. Chief Martin emerged from the driver's seat and opened the back, side door of the vehicle. Courtney jumped out and turned back to help Mr. Finch as he awkwardly stepped down from the van. Jenna, Angie, Euclid and Circe exited from the other side. Ellie made the decision to remain at the Victorian, claiming the B and B guests might need her.

This particular parking lot was used by the resort staff and delivery vehicles and was usually full during the day, but late in the evening, there were only several cars and a few trucks scattered around the spaces.

Chief Martin was dressed in chinos and a button-down shirt. Angie couldn't remember ever seeing him out of uniform. He chose the unmarked police van, civilian clothes, and the time of night to return to the murder scene with the Roseland sisters and Mr. Finch so as not to call attention to their visit. The chief led the way. "We can follow this walkway for a while and then branch off to the right. We'll end up at the luxury bungalows. You okay to walk a bit, Mr. Finch?"

"I'm not fast, but I can walk for some distance," Finch assured the chief.

Courtney held Finch's elbow and carried a flashlight in her other hand to provide better lighting as they moved along the stone walkways in the darkness. The cats walked slightly in front of them and Angie and Jenna carried up the rear.

Anticipation pinged in Angie's chest and her shoulder muscles tightened. She took a sideways glance at her sister wondering if she was experiencing any nervousness or worry.

The group wound around the resort grounds past shade trees, ornamental bushes and grasses, and flowers planted in beds and potted in containers. Subtle, decorative lighting enhanced the loveliness of the landscaping. Private bungalows were tucked here and there in the lush section of the resort. Angie knew that some of the cottages had private pools in the small fenced gardens behind the structures. Guests in this part of the resort could even request a personal butler to see to their needs.

Angie's stomach tightened as they approached the darkened crime scene bungalow. She tried to breathe slowly and evenly. The chief removed a key from his pocket, inserted it into the lock, and pushed the door open. He entered first and flicked the light switch to illuminate the room.

Everyone stepped into the elegant living space and the chief closed the door. The blinds had already been drawn to block out the curious gazes of passersby.

"So." The chief explained the layout to Mr. Finch since this was his first time in the cottage. The cats listened intently as the chief spoke about where and how Nelson Rider's body was found. "I have some other information to share when you are finished in here. I don't want to say anything that might influence what you ... ah, sense."

Jenna looked at the chief. "Were you able to bring the gun for Mr. Finch to touch?"

"The weapon cannot be removed from the evidence locker. I'm trying to gain access for you, Mr. Finch. It might take some time." The chief shoved his hands into his back pockets and shifted his eyes about the room. "I guess I'll go sit over by the door." He picked up a small wooden chair from next to the desk and carried it over to the front door, where he placed it, and sat down heavily.

The amateur sleuths stared at each for a few moments and then Angie made a suggestion. "Why don't we each walk around and try to pick up on anything." The others nodded and each one turned in a different direction. The cats had already begun to pad about the space.

Jenna was drawn to the bedroom where she'd

had a vision of a shadow the last time they inspected the premises. The linens had been removed from the bed and the mattress stood in the room, empty and bare. Something about the lonely scene caused grief to stick in Jenna's throat. She shook herself and took soft steps over to the bed. She placed her hand gingerly on the mattress, and waited.

Angie and Courtney walked slowly around the living room. Mr. Finch moved to the dining section of the bungalow. A good-sized table and six chairs stood in the center of the area. There was a decorative rug of muted colors on the floor under the dining table. Three windows looked out over the back garden and the small pool. A chandelier hung down from the ceiling. Mr. Finch shuffled around the perimeter of the table, running his hand over the wood's smooth finish.

Hearing a strange buzzing in her ears, Angie stopped beside the gas fireplace. The edges of her vision darkened and she pressed her fingers to her eyes. Flickers of light in the shape of lightning bolts zipped in her field of vision. She wondered if it was the beginning of a migraine and she groaned inwardly for not bringing headache meds with her. Everything seemed draped in fog. Her hearing became muffled.

There was a knock on the door. She turned to it. Another knock sounded. It wasn't hard and harsh like a man's fist hitting the wood. It was softer, the noise made by a woman's knuckles. Angie tried to tell the person to come in, but her throat was tight and no words could escape. She heard the metallic scratching of a key fitting into the lock. The doorknob turned and the door opened. Kim Hutchins entered and called for Nelson. She was unaware of Angie's presence.

Angie's vision dimmed to only a pinhole. Voices could be heard. Then the voices grew angry. Euclid and Circe faced the bedroom and hissed. Kim Hutchins raced out of Nelson's bedroom and hurried to leave the bungalow. The slam of the front door shook the cottage.

Angie's eyesight slowly returned and with it, a pounding headache. Chief Martin had his arm around her shoulders. He led her to the sofa.

"What happened?" Angie squeaked out the words.

"You stood like a statue. You seemed to be in a trance." Perspiration beaded on the chief's forehead.

Just then, Jenna stumbled out of the bedroom and made her way to the chair across from Angie. Her face looked rubbery and white. "Did you see something?"

Angie nodded. "I thought it was real, but it was just a vision."

Courtney, Mr. Finch, and the cats gathered around. Angie relayed what she'd seen.

"I had a vision too." Jenna took a deep breath.

"Nelson was on the bed. It seemed like he was sleeping. I heard two other people arguing. Then a shadow moved over Nelson. The shadow placed a pillow over his face. And then I heard the gunshot."

"Could you see the killer's face?" Chief Martin looked as pale as Jenna.

She shook her head.

Mr. Finch spoke next. "As I moved my hand over the dining table, I could feel energy there. I believe a bottle of pills spilled over and left a trace behind on the wood."

"Drugs. Pain killers, no doubt." Chief Martin's eyebrows knitted together. "Courtney? Anything?"

"I felt the thrumming. I had a flash of a vision. I saw the image of a blonde woman enter Nelson's bedroom. I could only see her from the back. She wore her hair up. I couldn't get a sense of her age or see who it was, but she held a gun." Courtney wrapped her arms around herself.

Euclid let out a hiss.

Chief Martin rubbed the side of his face. "We have some footage from the security camera in front of this bungalow. A woman is seen knocking on the door. Twice."

All eyes shot to Angie. It was what she'd seen in her vision.

"The woman then opens her purse and removes a phone. She places a call on her cell phone, but it seems that no one answers. She takes out a key and unlocks the door. She isn't inside for very long.

After a bit, she's seen hurrying from the bungalow. The images are terribly grainy and her features can't be seen clearly." The chief cleared his throat. "We obtained cell phone records for Kim Hutchins. As near as we can tell, which is pretty good, she placed a call to Nelson at the same time the woman outside Nelson's bungalow placed a call."

"It was Kim who knocked and then unlocked the door." Angie shook herself and rubbed her temple. "Was there any luck tracing all that money that went into Kim's account?"

"Not yet. It's a process that is very time-consuming."

"So it's looking pretty good that Kim killed Nelson." Courtney leaned back in the chair.

Circe was sitting on her lap. She let out a low guttural growl.

"Whoa, little one." Courtney patted the black cat's head. "Take it easy."

Jenna pondered. "Piecing it together, it seems that Kim must have been furious that Nelson derailed her career by not running for Senate and because he let her go from her job as his assistant because he had a thing for her that she did not reciprocate."

Courtney said, "Maybe Nelson gave Kim that huge amount of cash. Maybe he felt awful that he was damaging her career and wanted to help her by giving her money."

Angie's eyes narrowed. "The bartender said

Nelson got a call when he was sitting at the bar. He took the call and then left in a hurry. That was shortly before he was killed." She looked at the chief. "Can you find out who called him?"

"We know who called him. It was his Boston drug dealer arriving in Sweet Cove with a stash of pills for Nelson. Nelson had run out of his pain killers." The chief stood up, a scowl on his face. "I'll be talking with Kim Hutchins early in the morning."

As the group filed out of the bungalow into the darkness, Angie felt a sense of dread running through her veins. Something was off, but she couldn't quite put the puzzle pieces together.

CHAPTER 24

Angie borrowed Jenna's station wagon to make her early morning bakery deliveries. She couldn't wait to open her bake shop in the Victorian and be able to just walk down the stairs to work each morning. Backing out of the driveway, Angie saw the plainclothes police officer sitting in an unmarked car across from her house. He was there to keep an eye on Kim Hutchins until Chief Martin drove over to pick her up for questioning.

Zaps of electricity pulsed down Angie's spine. Heading to the resort, anxiety pounded in her chest and she didn't know why she couldn't shake the unease. It seemed clear that Kim was Nelson's killer. She had motive and opportunity and was seen entering and leaving the bungalow around the time that Nelson was killed. Then why did Angie feel something was wrong?

She blew out a long breath of air as she pulled into the resort and drove around to the delivery door. She parked and lifted the back hatch so that she could remove a long metal tray of baked treats.

She headed for the kitchen entrance. The door opened and a young man took the tray. A woman signed the receipt.

Angie had wanted to do something nice for Josh, so she'd made him his favorite dessert, a pear frangipane tart. She drove around to the front of the resort and carried the treat inside. She knew Josh was away on a short business trip and was returning later in the day, so she asked the concierge to place the tart in Josh's refrigerator.

Hurrying down the hallway to return to the parking lot, Angie passed the breakfast room and spotted Nelson's sister, Georgia Rider, sitting alone at a table sipping tea. Angie paused, and then making a decision, entered the stylish café where she walked over to Georgia's table and re-introduced herself. "May I join you?" When Georgia looked up, something like an icy cold finger skittered down Angie's back.

Georgia was dressed in a cream-colored linen skirt and jacket. Her white shirt had a small, diamond dragonfly pinned to the collar. She was wearing tortoise-shell glass frames. Her nails were the palest shade of pearly pink and her white-blonde bob was blow-dried to perfection.

In her blue skirt, sandals, and sleeveless yellow shirt, Angie felt like a frump standing next to the refined, successful businesswoman. Georgia's face showed recognition and she gestured to the chair opposite.

"I'm leaving right after breakfast. I'm flying back to New York." Georgia buttered her slice of toast, and then waved the waiter over to take Angie's order for tea.

"I had deliveries to make here." Angie explained her baking business which also seemed frumpy in light of Georgia being the CEO of a multi-national financial firm. "Did you fly up from New York the night Nelson died?"

The woman nodded. "Though technically, it was the next morning." Georgia seemed more elegant and restrained than she'd been at Nelson's remembrance service. Angie could picture her running a large company and controlling a boardroom. Georgia's phone buzzed and she checked the screen. "I must take this call. Excuse me." She rose and walked into the resort lobby to speak to the person on the phone.

Angie looked out the window. Her arms and legs felt twitchy. She squirmed in her seat. Something was picking at her. Something wasn't right. Her phone buzzed with a text message. It was Ellie. She and Jack Ford wanted to take the train up to Newburyport for some shopping and sightseeing in the historic district. They would return the following evening. Ellie wanted to know if Angie would be around to tend the B and B while she was gone. Angie replied that she'd be glad to help out and wished her sister a fun time. She placed her phone on the table just as Georgia returned and slid into her seat as easily as the last puzzle piece fits into its space and completes the picture.

The train.

Ellie's text about taking the train triggered the memory in Angie's mind of helping Georgia return items to her purse when she'd dropped it at the memorial service. There was a receipt for the train from New York to Boston. For the day *before* Nelson was killed.

Did Georgia Rider kill her brother?

An icy shudder ran down Angie's spine. When she looked across the table at the woman, she had to suppress a gasp. "I've lost track of time," Angie stammered. "I need to finish my deliveries." She tossed a few dollars on the table for the tea and rushed from the room. Hurrying to the car, she called Chief Martin and informed him of her idea about Georgia. Then she told him where she was headed next.

***

Angie swerved into the Victorian's driveway so fast that the tires squealed. The unmarked police car was parked at the curb so she knew Kim Hutchins was still inside. She jogged to the front porch, opened the door, and rushed into the foyer. Kim, sitting at the dining table, looked up in surprise when the young woman burst into the room.

Angie caught her breath. "You need to talk. Come into the sunroom with me." Not waiting to see if Kim would follow, she turned on her heel and hurried away through the living room to the other room. When Angie reached the sunroom, she saw Mr. Finch sitting by the windows reading. He looked up just as Kim came in behind her.

Finch stood and extended his hand. "Although we've seen each other coming and going, I don't believe we've formally met. Victor Finch."

Kim accepted the man's handshake. "Kim Hutchins."

Holding the woman's hand, Finch felt the jolt he was expecting. This was indeed the woman who had bashed him over the head at Nelson's memorial service. He raised an eyebrow to Angie and nodded.

"You need to be straight with us." Angie's voice was urgent. "Police Chief Martin will be here any minute. There is security camera footage of you at Nelson's bungalow shortly before he was killed."

"What do you want to know?" Kim's voice trembled.

"Perhaps you could start by explaining why you knocked me over the head." Finch placed both hands over the top of his cane.

Kim shook her head. "I didn't...."

"You may stop right there." Finch looked over the top of his eyeglasses. "The truth, please."

Kim sank onto the sofa just as Chief Martin entered the room, followed by Euclid and Circe. The cats leaped up onto the desk against the wall and turned their gaze on Kim. Angie was glad to see that neither feline hissed or growled as they watched the woman. Now she was sure that Kim Hutchins did not kill Nelson Rider.

The attractive blonde seemed so tiny sitting alone on the sofa. Her voice was but a whisper when she said, "I'd like to speak to the chief alone."

Angie blinked. She, the cats, and Mr. Finch headed out of the sunroom. Before they disappeared from view, Kim called to Finch, "I'm sorry about hitting you."

Finch turned back, gave a slight nod, and walked away.

***

The next afternoon, Ellie came in through the Victorian's front door looking happy and calm from her trip to Newburyport with Jack Ford. She spotted her sisters, the cats, and Mr. Finch sitting together in the living room and her face drooped. "What's happened now?"

"Plenty." Courtney called Ellie in to take a seat. "The killer has been caught."

"What?" Ellie sat in the side chair. "I leave for a day and everything is solved?"

Jenna smiled. "Angie figured it out."

"But only with your help." Angie nodded at Ellie.

"I wasn't even here. How did I help?" Ellie's forehead creased with confusion.

The group explained how Ellie's train trip had triggered Angie's memory of seeing Georgia's train receipt.

"Georgia claimed to have flown to Boston from New York on the corporate jet the morning after Nelson was killed. The jet flew from New York, but Georgia wasn't on it. She arranged for the company's plane to fly to Boston so that she could say she was a passenger. In fact, she took the train to Boston and arrived in Sweet Cove the day *before* the murder. She planned to kill her brother that very night," Jenna explained.

"But why?" Ellie's voice went up an octave.

Angie sighed. "Nelson refused to do Georgia's bidding any longer. He wasn't going to marry Bethany. He wasn't going to run for the Senate. He was done taking orders about his life. She was infuriated by his refusals and by his drug use since he wouldn't kick his habit. Georgia wasn't going to let him cause a scandal and embarrass the family or their company."

Mr. Finch picked up the story. "Kim Hutchins arrived at the bungalow that night. She had a key to the suite, given to her by the brother, Geoffrey, so she could check on Nelson. When she went inside, Georgia was there. Georgia claimed that

Nelson shot himself. She pretended to be distraught and asked Kim to move the gun from the bed to the dresser. When Kim touched the gun, Georgia sneered at her and told her that now Kim's fingerprints were the only ones on the weapon. Georgia had broken into the bungalow through the back window. She'd worn gloves to conceal her fingerprints."

Courtney continued the tale. "It was an added bonus that Nelson got high while Georgia was hiding in the bedroom waiting for him. Nelson made it easy for her. He took his drugs, lay down on the bed, fell asleep, and she shot him. Kim came in a few minutes later. Georgia threatened to bring the gun with Kim's fingerprints to the police. She told Kim she'd be the only one on the security tape since Georgia came and went through the back window. Kim was terrified of being accused of Nelson's murder. As an added incentive to make Kim seem guilty, Georgia had the large cash deposit credited to Kim's bank account."

"It made Kim look like she received a payoff for killing Nelson." Angie scratched Circe's cheek. "Georgia also sent those threatening letters to Todd Moore. She was trying to scare him away from Bethany."

Jenna sipped from her water glass. "The day Kim ran out of her room so suddenly was because Georgia wanted to speak with her about keeping quiet. She told Kim to come to the rental mansion right away or she would tell the police Kim was the killer. Georgia was staying at the mansion as Senator Winston's guest. She made the company's human resource manager make all the calls to Kim so there was no trace of contact from Georgia."

Angie sighed. "Chief Martin arrested Georgia for her brother's murder. Charges will be filed against Kim, but they will probably be minor due to Georgia threatening her."

Mr. Finch said, "Miss Hutchins admitted to hitting me in a panic. Ms. Georgia Rider had the murder weapon at the memorial. At an opportune moment, she placed the gun in Miss Kim's purse, and then made the anonymous call to the police. When Kim opened her handbag and saw the gun, she panicked, and tried to find a place to hide it at the rental mansion. I interrupted her and she struck me with the fireplace poker."

"Good grief." Ellie shook her head slowly. "We got sucked into this whole mess because the Winston's hired us for their wedding." She exhaled. "No more wedding events for us. They're too much trouble."

The three sisters and Mr. Finch made eye contact with one another and smiled.

Courtney giggled. "It's too late. We're already involved in a new wedding."

Ellie was dumbfounded and looked at the others wondering what was going on. "How? I was only away for a day."

Everyone chuckled.
The cats trilled.

CHAPTER 25

The early evening sky mimicked the beauty and color of Ellie's backyard flower gardens, with streaks of pink and lavender against the blue. White fluffy clouds passed high overhead. The pergola had been decorated with garlands of flowers, flowing diaphanous fabric, and baby-blue and pink colored ribbons. White wooden folding chairs were placed in two groups in front of the patio trellises. The lawn had been freshly mowed and the gardens spilled over with fragrant blossoms.

Angie wore her apron over her pale pink dress. She bent to place white roses on each layer of the wedding cake making them seem like a flowing waterfall curving along the side of the confection. She pushed some strands of hair away from her face with the back of her hand and reached for the pastry bag to pipe some decorative bits of frosting around the flowers.

Courtney came into the kitchen for some silverware. "Whoa. That cake is gorgeous." She wore her honey hair half up and half down and had on a soft yellow sleeveless dress that flowed around her ankles. Gold colored heels completed her outfit.

Tom and Rufus came in looking handsome in their suits. Angie gave them instructions on how to safely carry the cake out to the garden. She followed behind clucking suggestions as they inched their way down the back stairs carrying the masterpiece to the small cake table.

The four piece string quartet arrived and set up to the side on the lawn. Four people arrived that the Roselands didn't know and introductions were made. One of the young women went inside the carriage house to the second floor apartment, just as Mr. Finch came over the property line from his house, arm and arm with Betty Hayes.

"You're looking very dapper in your new suit, Mr. Finch." Courtney beamed at the man. Finch had purchased a summer-weight light gray suit for the occasion.

Jack Ford and Josh Williams came down the driveway of the Victorian, both looking handsome as usual. Ellie gave Jack a hug while Josh hurried over to give Angie a sweet kiss.

Tom had just finished lighting the torches that ringed the perimeter of the gardens when Jenna emerged from the carriage house wearing a soft blue dress, silver earrings, and silver sandals. "Everything's ready now. It's time to start."

Police Chief Martin and his wife Lucille hurried around the corner of the house and took their seats in the back row. Mr. Finch who turned out to be a Justice of the Peace, leaned on his cane and walked to the center of the pergola where he turned to face the small gathering.

Circe, wearing a delicate powder blue ribbon tied in a bow around her neck, and Euclid, with a tiny dark blue bow tie under his chin, jumped up on one of the white chairs in the front row and the two sat side-by-side.

Todd Moore, wearing a gray suit with a small, red rose pinned to his lapel, took his place under the pergola next to Mr. Finch. The quartet began to play and the guests stood and turned to watch the bride approach.

Bethany Winston appeared at the side of the carriage house. Her platinum blonde hair was high on her head in an elegant bun, her soft bangs swept to the side. Her white silk dress skimmed the tops of her pink sandals and she held a small bouquet of pink, red, and white roses courtesy of Ellie's garden. A necklace of crystals and pearls, designed by Jenna, hung elegantly around Beth's neck.

A soft smile played over her face when she made eye contact with Todd across the lawn. She took slow steps down the flower-strewn aisle between the rows of chairs to the pergola where Todd greeted her with a kiss. They turned to Mr. Finch.

"Dearly beloved," Mr. Finch began the

ceremony.

When the rings had been exchanged and the couple named husband and wife, Mr. Finch closed the rites by saying, "What love has joined together, let no one put asunder."

As the newly-married couple kissed, the love between the two of them seemed to float on the air, and Angie could feel the atoms around them swirling with sweetness and light. At the very same moment, Courtney and Angie sighed with happiness. The sisters looked at each other and chuckled.

Bethany and Todd had wanted a small private ceremony and invited only three close friends and Todd's brother to attend. Beth would tell her father sometime in the coming weeks and if he accepted her choice and wanted to host a large reception for them, they would not be opposed, but today was for them and an intimate gathering was the way they wanted to begin their lives together.

The guests feasted on a buffet of chili-lime chicken breast, pulled pork, red bliss potato salad, fresh corn and summer pea salad, and a mandarin orange, strawberry, and mesclun salad with raspberry vinaigrette. There was a bar set up with glass jars of iced tea, lemonade, and sparkling water, and with a variety of beers, wines, and champagne available. A table next to the wedding cake held individual dessert glasses filled with mini scoops of lemon, lime, and mango sorbet. Everyone enjoyed their meals sitting at round tables draped with white table cloths and decorated with vases of colorful flowers and flickering candles set in small white lanterns.

After the event was over, and Bethany and Todd had driven away, Ellie suggested that they all sit on the front porch with tea or coffee before any clean-up started. Ellie carried a tray with cups and saucers out to the porch and everyone settled in the porch rockers while Angie went to the kitchen to put the water on and brew the coffee.

Waiting for the beverages, Angie started to rinse some plates in the sink. She glanced out the window and saw Jenna and Tom standing under the pergola, talking. Suddenly, Tom took Jenna's hand and got down on one knee.

Angie gasped. Her hand flew up to her mouth. Smiling, she spun around away from the window to give her sister and Tom their private moment. Tears of happiness gathered in her eyes. She brushed at them and carried the tea and coffee out to the front porch.

The sisters and their beaus, and Mr. Finch and Betty sat chatting and rocking when the Victorian's front door opened and Jenna and Tom came out to the porch. Tom stood straight and tall with a goofy grin on his face. Jenna's cheeks had a flush of pink and her lips turned up in a sweet smile. Tom cleared his throat. "We have something to say." All eyes turned to the couple.

"Jenna has agreed to marry me." He looked lovingly at the brunette gazing up at him. "I am now the happiest man on Earth." He hugged her tightly.

Courtney whooped.

Euclid and Circe trilled with joy.

Everyone stood, shook hands, hugged, and offered congratulations to Jenna and Tom.

"A wedding and an engagement all in the same day." Ellie marveled at the happy events.

Jenna held out her hand to show her engagement ring. The small lovely diamond set in a white gold band had been Tom's grandmother's ring.

"I love it." Jenna beamed.

"We've decided on a long engagement," Tom said. "A house on Beach Street is coming on the market soon." He nodded to Betty. "I've already talked with Betty about helping me with the purchase."

"Which house?" Courtney asked.

"Two houses down from this one. The old abandoned Queen Anne place. Set back from the road, overgrown with bushes and trees." Tom smiled at Jenna. "I'm going to buy it and restore it for us. Jenna has approved the idea." He looked at the people standing with them on the porch. "I can't have Jenna too far from her sisters and friends. And to be honest, I don't want to be far from you either. I don't have any family, my parents are gone, no siblings. I've come to think of all of you as my family." Tom had to clear his throat.

Angie could see a few tears in the corners of the big man's eyes and her heart swelled.

Tom placed his burly hand softly against Jenna's cheek, bent down, and kissed her under the golden light of the Victorian's porch lamp, surrounded by everyone they loved.

THANK YOU FOR READING!

BOOKS BY J.A. WHITING CAN BE
FOUND HERE:

www.amazon.com/author/jawhiting

To hear about new books and book
sales, please sign up for my mailing list
at:

www.jawhitingbooks.com

Your email will never be sold, shared, or
spammed.

COZY MYSTERIES

The Sweet Dreams Bake Shop (Sweet Cove Cozy
Mystery Book 1)
Murder So Sweet (Sweet Cove Cozy Mystery Book
2)
Sweet Secrets (Sweet Cove Cozy Mystery Book 3)
Sweet Deceit (Sweet Cove Cozy Mystery Book 4)
*Sweetness and Light (Sweet Cove Cozy Mystery
Book 5)*

And more to come!

MYSTERIES

The Killings (Olivia Miller Mystery – Book 1)
Red Julie (Olivia Miller Mystery - Book 2)
The Stone of Sadness (Olivia Miller Mystery - Book 3)
Justice (Olivia Miller Mystery - Book 4) Coming Soon
Summoning the Earth (Olivia Miller Mystery - Book 5) Coming Soon

If you enjoyed the book, please consider leaving a review.

A few words are all that's needed.

It would be very much appreciated.

ABOUT THE AUTHOR

J.A. Whiting lives with her family in New England where she works full time in education. Whiting loves reading and writing mystery, suspense and thriller stories.

VISIT ME AT:

www.jawhitingbooks.com

www.facebook.com/jawhitingauthor

www.amazon.com/author/jawhiting

SOME RECIPES FROM THE SWEET COVE SERIES

BLUEBERRY AND LEMON TART

Ingredients for the Pastry

* 1½ cups of all-purpose flour
* 1½ Tablespoons sugar
* a pinch of salt
* 1 stick unsalted butter (1/2 cup) – room temperature
* 1 egg
* 2 – 3 Tablespoons of cold water
* 1 egg white
* 1 teaspoon water

Ingredients for the Filling

* 4 eggs
* 1¼ cup sugar
* 5 - 6 lemons (to make a cup of lemon juice)
* ¼ - ⅓ cup heavy cream
* pinch of salt
* zest of 1 lemon
* 1 pint of blueberries

Directions for the Pastry

* In a bowl, mix flour, sugar, and salt together

*Add butter; mix together well

*Add the egg and the cold water and mix until it makes a nicely formed dough

* Wrap the dough in plastic wrap and refrigerate for 30 minutes.

* Roll the dough on a lightly floured surface; make about a 12-inch circle

* Use the rolling pin to roll the dough onto it; Lay the dough into a 10-inch tart pan (with removable bottom)

* Press the dough into the edges of the pan and fold the extra dough over to strengthen the rim

* Cover the tart pan with plastic wrap; Refrigerate for 30 minutes.

* Heat the oven to 350 degrees F

* **Place the tart pan on a baking sheet; Prick the bottom of the dough with a fork**

* **Cover the shell with a piece of parchment paper**

* **Bake for 25 minutes**

* **Remove the parchment paper**

* **Beat an egg white with 1 teaspoon water; Brush it onto the bottom and the sides of the tart shell**

Directions for the Filling

* **Whisk the eggs, sugar, lemon juice, cream, and lemon zest together**

* **Rinse and dry the blueberries. Add them to the cooled tart shell**

* **Pour the filling over the blueberries**

* **Bake for 20 to 25 minutes in 350 degrees F**

* **When done, the filling should jiggle a bit**

* **Let cool; remove from the tart pan**

Enjoy !

SHORT BREAD WEDGES

Makes 12 wedges

Ingredients

* ½ cup (1 stick) unsalted butter (room temperature)
* ½ cup confectioners' sugar
* 1 cup all-purpose flour
* ¼ teaspoon kosher salt
* ¼ cup light brown sugar

Directions

* Heat oven to 325° F

* Using a mixer, beat the butter and sugar on medium-high until light and fluffy (2 to 3 minutes)

* Reduce mixer speed to low; gradually add the flour and salt, mix until incorporated

*Dip fingers in flour; Press the dough into an 8-inch round cake pan

*Use a knife to mark the top of the dough into 12 wedges; Prick all over the dough with a toothpick

*Sprinkle dough with the light brown sugar

*Bake until golden and firm — about 35 to 40 minutes

*When cool, turn the shortbread out of the pan

*Use a knife (serrated works best) to re-cut along the lines to create the wedges

TOFFEE AND DARK CHOCOLATE FUDGE

Ingredients

* 1 tablespoon unsalted butter
* A 14-ounce can sweetened condensed milk
* 1 bag of dark chocolate chips
* 1 teaspoon sea salt, and a little more to garnish
* ½ cup toffee bits, and a little more to garnish

Directions

*Line an 8x8" baking dish with waxed paper and butter the paper

*Place the butter and sweetened condensed milk in a medium saucepan

*Heat the butter and condensed milk over medium-low heat until

blended together, stirring occasionally

*Remove from the heat and add the chocolate and a teaspoon of sea salt, stirring until smooth

*Add ½ cup toffee bits and stir until mixed

*Pour the mixture into the prepared pan; spread evenly with a spatula

*Press some toffee bits on top of the fudge, sprinkle sea salt on top (if desired)

*Chill 2 hours or until set

*Once the fudge has set, remove it from the pan and place on a cutting board

*Cut into small squares (use a sharp knife)

*Store in an airtight container in the refrigerator

Makes 36 small squares

YUMMY BANANA BREAD

Ingredients

* 3 ripe bananas
* 2 eggs
* 1 ¾ cups flour
* 1 ⅓ cups sugar
* ½ cup vegetable oil
* ¼ cup of milk
* 1 teaspoon of baking soda
* 1 teaspoon of vanilla
* ⅓ – ½ cup of chopped walnuts (if desired)

Directions

* In a bowl, mix together oil, eggs, sugar, and milk

*Mix in the vanilla and mashed bananas until combined

* Add the baking soda and flour and mix (about 2-3 minutes)

* If using nuts, add and combine into the banana mixture

* **Pour into the greased loaf pan**

***Bake in a preheated 325 degree F oven for 1 hour and 20 minutes or until a toothpick inserted in the center comes out clean**

LEMON AND CHILI CHICKEN

Ingredients

* 6 chicken breasts
* ¼ cup extra virgin olive oil
* 2 fresh lemons
* 3 cloves garlic, crushed
* ½ tbsp chili powder (for mild flavor)
* 1 tsp red chili pepper flakes
* Salt and pepper, to taste

Directions

*Place chicken breasts in a single layer in a roasting pan or dish; sprinkle with salt and pepper

*In a small bowl, zest the two lemons; cut them in half and squeeze their juice into the bowl

*Add olive oil, garlic, chili powder and chili pepper flakes. Whisk together until combined

*Pour marinade over the top of the breasts

*Cover the dish with plastic wrap and refrigerate for 1½ -2 hours

*Preheat the oven to 375 degrees F

*Remove the plastic wrap and cover the roasting pan or dish tightly with foil. Cut a few slits in the foil around the edges to vent

*Place chicken in the oven and cook for about 1 hour, until the internal temperature reaches 170 degrees F

*Remove the foil; Raise the oven temperature to 425 degrees F

*Bake the chicken for about 10 more minutes

Made in the USA
Las Vegas, NV
23 December 2024